#LoveBelievers
A Romance
Collection

A.A Schenna

Solstice Publishing - www.solsticepublishing.com

#LoveBelievers

A Romance Collection

A.A. Schenna

Table of Contents

5   A Woman's Heart

21   Live to Tell

30   Le Bal des Abeilles

45   Lullaby

52   Limitless Love Collection

74   On the Sixth Floor

107   What She Needs

166   The Stranger

A Woman's Heart

I leaned against the white wall and half-closed my eyes while struggling to stay calm and hoping she would make the right decision. I took a deep breath and looked up at the white ceiling as my hands kept shaking. I couldn't stop thinking of the loss, nor could I make up my mind immediately, acting like a real man, without fighting back tears.

The moment I heard the footsteps of the aged woman behind me, I froze in fear and couldn't think clearly. I wasn't sure what I wanted to hear, I didn't know what to expect since I was certain she would have to tell me the news which would define the rest of my life, and I would remain responsible for my careless action forever. The smell of the hospital and the big hall would haunt my memory for the next many weeks, months and years.

I always trusted my instincts and already knew I had made the worst mistake of my life. I would regret my hesitation; I should have done something to prevent this from happening. I should dare to fight against my vanity and selfishness because I truly loved her. If only I had acted drastically earlier.

"Mr. Pears," the nurse whispered and looked into my eyes while she shook her head. In no time I felt embarrassed, I knew I was a coward who had decided to run away from the problem I had caused and didn't have the intention to deal with it.

"Yes," I murmured. I felt like a criminal; I felt like being the most disgusting person on earth. Moreover, I sensed her words and her thoughts while I also felt that I had to apologize for not being mature. I had turned red, and soon, I started avoiding the nurse's sight. Yes, I was a coward and the worst person because I was still looking forward to running into relief.

The aged woman pulled her long, black hair away from her pale face and smiled at me, giving me the courage to let my speech free, making me feel relaxed and ready to accept reality. I guessed she realized that I needed support, and moreover, I had the desperate need to hear from someone that everything would get better and things would change. I bit my lips and did my best to hold my tears since I was ready to cry like a little boy who had screwed up everything just because there were rules I hadn't followed.

"You look like my son; he is just like you. Leo is in his early twenties and he thinks he knows everything. He is tall, muscular with big blue eyes like yours, but he is not ready to meet the challenges of life yet," she said with a little laugh as I was sure I would never forget her words. I averted my eyes and tried to find the strength to ask a question about my partner since my girl was going through hell, and even now, I hoped I would wake up and things would be the same as usual. I still wanted to find the secret path to heaven and limitless love again, and although I was face to face with the biggest challenge of my life, I dreamed of being somewhere else. I wished I was a bird, a free bird. If only I could fly high and get away from everything as soon as I could.

Instead, I came back to reality and decided that it was the time to confront the consequences of my own actions and stupid decisions.

"How is she?" I asked vaguely.

"I am afraid it's too late to change things," the nurse said and pulled her black hair back, leaving me alone. Some doctors were calling out for her and she left my side. I was confused. I wanted to scream.

I took a deep breath and took a few steps toward the empty blue seats. I closed my eyes and placed my hands on my face trying to hide my guilt and the tears of our loss.

The following minutes I kept looking around me, seeking my girl, watching the patients and the aged people who had fixed their eyes on me and waited for my reaction in silence. In a flash I realized that I needed someone to help me recover from the biggest shock of my life, and I didn't stop thinking about the way Ashley would feel after giving an end to the beginning of everything.

I stood up and walked toward the sealed window of the hall where I knelt and ignored everyone's presence, knowing they were all paying attention to me. The tears started running down my face as I was trying to heal the pain in my soul by asking forgiveness from God, praying to help me and Ashley overcome the tragedy we had caused. I was certain that nothing would be the same again between us since I had managed to let her down. I had proved that I wasn't the man she looked for because I wasn't there for Ashley like the way I should have been, and I felt responsible for everything. I couldn't stop the bleeding of my heart and I wasn't prepared to deal with her disappointment.

***

"I love this song," Ashley would never stop admiring Phil Collins. *Another Day In Paradise* was her favorite song and she always used to sing the lyrics along with the singer. And every time she used to stare and smile at me spreading the cover of her pure and limitless love in our shelter.

"I love you, and Phil Collins." I kissed her lips and felt like coming closer to heaven. Her kiss was the medicine to cure every doubt and whisper. Her smile was the most effective weapon against the insecurities which were looking for a chance to come up and dig up the fear of living with the same person forever. I hadn't realized that I was the happiest man on earth.

"I love you too." Ashley hugged me and didn't stop kissing me while I had gotten past the nasty voices in my head, hoping that we would remain like this for the rest of our lives. That period we had everything we needed and I wasn't able to respect and appreciate the vital affection of her presence in my empty life. Pure emotions, harmony, limitless love and strong feelings were the first elements that gave birth to life and humanity.

The oppressive heat and the shinning stars had managed to seduce our minds as our bodies carried on searching for the path the absolute pleasure, to euphoria. The smell of the red roses kept spreading through our cramped apartment while the sweat continued running down our bodies. She was mine, she belonged to me and she would do anything to see me happy. By the way she was looking at me, I could tell she would die for me and she didn't care whether I would do the same thing for her or not. The truth was that I would die for her too, but I never thought I should mention my confession. As usual, I refrained from speaking up and sharing my feelings with my beloved partner.

The unique atmosphere had made us impatient to taste the leaps of our mutual love. We made love again, sharing happiness and holding tight one another, knowing we had something special. Nevertheless, we would remain silent, hiding the secrets of our souls and the dark thoughts of our minds.

We had just finished our studies and we looked forward to making our plans for the future. Although, since I met my girl, I knew I wanted to share the rest of my life with Ashley, in time I started feeling weird. As time passed by, I realized I was getting more and more confused about my life and our relationship.

I could still remember our first night in our new home and the celebration of our graduation. That beautiful night would mark every single cell of my memory.

We liked talking about the past and I would never forget our first meeting and the way we came closer. One book and, specifically, the beautiful library at the college helped us find out that we were meant to be together. Soon, we discovered that we loved the same authors, the same music and the same movies. I couldn't describe the way she made me feel—it was unbelievable. She loved flowers and every time I came back home, I used to bring her the most beautiful red roses. But this was not enough, no; I had to act like a fool and destroy everything.

After four years of love, respect and appreciation, we would both discover the truth and, unfortunately, we would run into disappointment and anger. If only we knew…

***

"I have some great news," I said and immediately I locked Ashley in my hands and didn't let her go. I couldn't stop smiling.

"I have some great news too!" Ashley said, and I was surprised.

My girl wanted to believe that I would be thrilled. She kissed me and we walked to the sofa, hand in hand, impatient to share the good news. We sat down and Ashley was acting weird since she didn't seek my hug as usual. She wasn't sure about my reaction; she didn't insist on looking into my eyes as she always did.

"Tell me," I said.

"No, you will tell me first," Ashley was curious and hesitant. She placed her hands on my cheeks and I realized that she was shaking, she was anxious while the insecurities had started covering her thoughts. I ignored my instincts and moved on.

"I had a call from the J.S. office and next Friday I will discuss the details for my new job with the big boss," I said while I leaned over her side, trying to steal a kiss from her lips.

"That's great! I'm so happy!" Ashley hugged me tight and seemed to be really proud of me. My partner loved seeing me happy and she was waiting patiently to see me coming across success, although she was sure that one day I would become a successful lawyer.

"Now it's your turn. I want to hear everything." At first, I thought Ashley had found a job too. My beautiful lady adored English literature and I believed she was offered a job at the D.A School.

"I'm pregnant," Ashley said at once and I froze. I stood up from the sofa and she did the same thing too. I paralyzed and didn't know what to say. I looked into her big eyes and stopped smiling as Ashley stepped back and waited for my reaction, an answer, a few words that would make her feel secure. But I was shocked.

"Won't you say something?" Ashley asked me.

"I'm surprised," I managed to whisper.

Ashley took a few steps and walked to the large window of the small living room. The long black dress she wore had managed to cover the sorrow of her soul as the dark had already haunted her thoughts and had spread above the entire city.

Ashley looked up at the sky and let the stars watch her tears. Her long, blonde hair kept hiding her back and the bleeding of her heart, while the teardrops kept running down her sweet face, knowing already my answer and feelings.

Then again, I remained steady, feeling lost in my thoughts, watching in silence the reflection of the woman I loved on the cold glass of the window.

In a flash, we both felt like strangers to each other and I was responsible for the freezing situation. The most beautiful and sweet moments of our relationship had turned into ash and we could nothing to stop the destruction of everything we had struggled to create. We could do nothing to retain the emotional stability we both needed to deal with the biggest challenge life had brought in our lives.

I was still surprised, unprepared to face up the most critical fact of my life. I had no idea what to do. Normally, a glance at her big, bright blue eyes would help me overcome the initial shock, but Ashley was taken aback by my reaction and didn't turn back. My partner felt exposed, Ashley felt naked in front of a stranger and she felt guilt. She didn't have the courage to look back, to look into my eyes and tell me that I had betrayed her love and trust. And I was still there, speechless, as much a coward and fool as a little boy who needed his parents to take over.

***

It was the first weekend Ashley would stay alone. She had left our apartment and had decided to get away from me, the man she was sure she would always trust and would never abandon.

The small room in the beautiful hotel had become her shelter and the coastal town had managed to help her get past my reaction and refrain from panic as well. The sea and the walks on the beach had helped her pull herself back together and had also helped her make her decisions.

September was one of her favorite months since she always used to schedule everything for the next year. This time, Ashley would have to think seriously about her options, and she would have to make her plans based on her instincts and feelings because her decisions would define her future.

On the other hand, I had decided to give Ashley some time to consider the entire situation, without having my presence and my affection. I believed Ashley needed time to think of our options, ignoring the fact that I should have insisted on being next to her side, discussing everything concerning our futures. Later, after many years, I found out that I was wrong. Yes, I should have made my presence obvious. I shouldn't have been interested only for me while feeing lost and exposed.

***

The moment I heard the sound of my cell phone, I rushed to answer the call.

"What do you want? Do you want the baby?" Ashley asked while she tried to remain calm. Her voice was different. I was sure she was crying.

"I don't know," I whispered as Ashley swept the tears away and rolled her eyes.

"I talked to the doctor. Next Friday I'll be at J.C hospital." Ashley put the phone down and laid on the bed. I placed the glass of the red wine on the small table. I sank in my favorite chair and rubbed my eyes, thinking of my beloved partner and our options.

The night had dressed the beautiful town as the white color of the walls and the yellow curtains had stolen Ashley's attention while struggling to find the light in her soul again. I had turned her life and dreams into ruins and she would never forgive me for my indifference.

***

Ashley was sure she had sent the email, she was sure I had received the messages she had sent me. She waited for me, but in vain. I had made my decisions and she would make hers.

I was aware of the meeting with the doctor, but I had to meet the big boss to discuss the details about my job as well. I was flirting with the most critical dilemma in my life; I had had to decide about my life and future. I would never overcome the loss of my baby, but I didn't want to postpone or even reject my appointment with money, fame and success too. I was stupid, I was selfish, the worst person on earth because I had never realized I had the power of love. Ashley was my secret power and I had betrayed her the moment she really needed my support. I was young, fool and naïve.

***

"Are you ready?" The doctor asked Ashley.

"Yes, I am." The nurse nodded at Ashley and walked out of the small room to let her take off her clothes.

Ashley blinked her eyes and shook her head as the tears started running down her face. She was trying to find the pieces of her shattered soul and she had no one standing by her side. She never thought she would come across the experience of killing a baby, but she regarded it was the only way to get past my betrayal and dangerous presence from her life forever. She didn't want to see me again and she told that to the aged nurse who guided her to the lifeless room. I would never forget the day I had left my boss's office to find Ashley and I would never forget the nurse's words before leaving my side.

"She doesn't want to see you again," she had told me before hearing the panicked doctors who were seeking for help and for the most experienced nurses to save another baby who needed their immediate action. It was the last time I was near her presence and it was my first day off from my new job. I had lost my personal happiness but that time I believed I would find her again after she would find herself back and reorganize her priorities. But deep inside my soul, I was sure I was wrong. I had lost her.

***

Ashley would never miss the graduation of her son. She was so proud of him and she couldn't control her feelings and tears. She was always focused on her son's needs, ignoring living her own life and having some fun with her friends and another partner. Ashley had remained a beautiful woman and had still the ability to steal everyone's attention. Ageless beauty—two words were enough to describe her picture.

The moment she saw her son graduating, she couldn't prevent the tears from making their appearance on her sweet face again. Ashley looked back, and out of the blue, she took a deep breath wondering about my presence at the college. She looked back again and seemed to worry about the way things would evolve since she had big plans and nothing would destroy her mood, not even the man she had trusted in the past, her first love, and the father of her precious baby.

The firm I worked for would hire the best new lawyers and Ashley's son would become one of the best lawyers I would meet.

"This is my Mom, Ashley Sterns. Mom, this is Jonathan Lee," Steve said as Ashley offered her hand and pretended she didn't know me.

"Pleased to meet you," she said and later she left me alone with my son. It was not difficult to realize that the young man I was looking at was my son. I stayed calm and pretended I was just a stranger while I really wanted to hug my son and tell him that I was sorry for not being in his life, next to his mother's side.

I was single, in my early fifties and I had nothing but fame and money. I had missed the chance to experience the birth and the raise of my own child because I thought success and wealth would make me happy. Ashley had done everything, while in truth, I never tried to find her. I waited for her and I never dared to pick up the phone and call her.

If I could turn back the time, I would change everything. But, now, it was too late to think about it. I had to adjust to reality and thank the woman I had betrayed for showing me the real meaning of life. Ashley had taught me what love meant in silence, from distance and always remained a special lady. There was no one who had managed to steal her heart except me; she never trusted anyone else because of me. She met a lot of men, but she never gave them the key of her heart, as I never gave the key of my heart to any other woman. And now, I could see the key of my future in front of me. At some point, I noticed Ashley gazing at me and I sensed her eyes penetrating my soul. Her big eyes were wondering about my behavior. I felt like a fugitive, but I didn't run. Not this time. I would do anything and I couldn't wait for too long to get into their lives.

***

I closed the door of my big house and sank in my favorite sofa. I had closed the door to happiness because I was a fool, but I was lucky to find my son. Steve had accepted my apology and liked having me in his life. I was so happy I had met my son and I was glad that he was a good young man. Steve was a cool guy with great manners and healthy aspirations.

I looked up at the sky and waved at the beautiful birds which loved making circles around the yellow tile roof, considering the most beautiful things in life. I could smell the snow and I felt nice when I saw the city lights and the Christmas trees. The whole place looked incredible, and after many years I finally realized the reason so many families loved Christmas and the rest holidays.

I tried to breathe normally and placed my hands on my chest. I closed my eyes and I felt that the bleeding of my heart had stopped. I wanted to do something for my son and Ashley. I wanted to feel like all the other people. I needed to feel I belonged to a family, even though I hadn't done anything earlier to earn their love and respect.

***

In a few hours I had done everything. I had visited all the places I wanted, and now I was outside Ashley's house, ready to spend my first night with my family. Christmas Eve and everyone was home, sharing beautiful moments with those they really wanted and loved.

The moment I stood outside the door, I hesitated. I wanted so badly and desperately to ring the bell, I felt my heart ready to jump from its position to leave my body and live me standing there lifeless. I wasn't going to step back, not this time.

"Merry Christmas," I said and kept shaking, waiting for my son's answer.

"Merry Christmas, Dad," Steve said and I felt like a bird, like a free bird.

"This is so big…"

Steve looked at the tree and seemed amazed. I had bought the biggest and the most expensive tree I had seen and I had made it, my son liked it. He really did.

"Who is…" Ashley froze.

"Merry Christmas," I said and she smiled at me.

"Merry Christmas," Ashley said and watched Steve helping his father carry the tree.

"It's too big for our house," Ashley whispered and stared at the two men.

"It's too big for all the houses in the neighborhood," Steve said and laughed.

I was living the most intense and the happiest moments of my life. I was with the woman I was always in love and we had our son watching us. If only I could change things, if only I could turn back the time.

"Thank you for all the presents, but you shouldn't have gotten into this whole trouble." Steve was kind and felt nice seeing me there. He liked his new iphone and his laptop. On the other hand, Ashley didn't seem impressed. I had bought her favorite perfume and she didn't say anything, she nodded and then she hid in the kitchen of the spacious, beautiful house.

"I wish I knew everything earlier, I would have done much more." I said while Ashley came back and sat down next to us. Then, she hooked her gaze on me, ready to speak up.

"Everything is complicated, but I don't think it's the time to discuss it again, and especially right now, this day." Ashley smiled and didn't add anything further.

"You'll stay with us for dinner, won't you?" Steve asked me and I couldn't find the exact words to describe my joy.

"Are you going to be alone?" I said and looked at Ashley.

"You could stay if you want," She said and got up from her seat and walked toward the kitchen again.

"It's just the two of us, like many, many years." Steve said and laughed. He was happy, I was sure he was glad seeing me in their living room.

"Have you decided?" Ashley asked from the kitchen and she reminded me of the girl I was living with during our college years when we used to spend Christmas and the rest holidays together in our cramped, sweet home.

"I think I'll stay," I said and Steve smiled at me.

"I'm glad you are here with us, dad." Steve whispered and then came closer to me.

"It's nice being here." Steve hugged me and I held him in my arms. Oh gosh, I really missed that feeling.

"I am so happy I am here with you and your mother, son. I love you so much and thank you," I whispered as I swept the tears away.

"I love you too, dad."

I was lucky because I had the best son in the whole world. In a few months we had gotten to know each other well and his mother never tried to destroy our relationship. I had earned my son's trust and I was determined to never let him or his mother down again. They were the only people I had in my life and they had forgiven me.

"I think we are ready. Dinner is on the table," Ashley said and pointed at the dining room, smiling at me and our son.

"Smells wonderful," I said and we all headed toward the table.

***

"So you are leaving us," I said as I could see Steve ready to leave the house. He had his plans and he really liked parties.

"I heard it's going to be the best party in town," he answered and waved his hand.

"Have fun," I said.

"I will."

"Don't drink too much and drive safe." Ashley sounded worried. She didn't like the weather and the snow.

"I'll be fine, Mom. You two have fun as well!"

When Steve closed the door and got into his car, my eyes focused on hers. It was like living the same night at our new home after our graduation. She looked like she wanted to tell me something.

"I hope I didn't destroy your plans," I said and she gazed at me.

"No, Jonathan, you didn't destroy my plans." Ashley said.

"I am sorry I invaded your house, I should have asked you first,"

"It's okay," she said.

"Ashley, I am sorry." I thought I ought to say it.

"Jonathan, it is okay, I have already forgiven you." she said.

"I was afraid," I confessed and looked into her eyes.

"Now I know it," Ashley whispered and I held her hand.

"I was afraid we wouldn't make it," I cried out and Ashley swept my tears.

"Now I know who you really are, Jonathan." Tears ran down her cheeks and I caressed her sweet face.

"I am sorry for all the adventure you went through."

"It's okay, now everything is good," Ashley whispered and hid in my hug, looking for a place to feel safe and let her soul feel secure.

"Do you want me in your life?" I asked.

"Yes, I want you, we both want you."

"I am so glad to hear this."

We sat in front of the fireplace, watching the Christmas tree and the snowflakes. We had missed feeling nice, we had forgotten all the good things, and Christmas was the best time to feel all the joy and optimism of the universe.

Confessions, secrets, and plans were revealed. We decided to make a new beginning where we would all respect one another and be honest. We would never hide our true feelings and we would never afraid exposing our emotions. Ashley was the strongest woman I had ever met and I was lucky she had decided to keep my baby. I had turned her down and she didn't kick me out of her house. I had hurt her and she didn't hurt me back because she loved people and she knew I was weak. I was lucky because I had lived the best Christmas in my life in a beautiful place that felt like home and I had the chance to realize the meaning of this day.

When you really love someone, you have to try to forgive them. No one is perfect and none will ever be. Share the love and you will get everything you need and seek. It happened to me. It could happen to you too.

Live to Tell

Cultivate your heart with the seed of selflessness and you will see our society changing. Your soul will spread the love through the world like the air we breathe.

A.A Schenna

No one seemed to care about what had made us all different. We had decided to focus on taking care of ourselves while killing hopes, destroying plans and changing the lives of countless of innocent people who were searching for all those humanity will always look for.

True love, hope and positive energy had vanished for the sake of money and stupid glory. Vanity had won the battle against happiness and carefree living while the feelings of euphoria were trapped behind the increasing shape of selfish hearts and tainted love.

Lovers had come face-to-face with the nightmare of the urban living since they had to survive in a modern society where the lack of a good job, money and independence kept stealing their energy and taking back their hopes for a safer, peaceful future and a better world. Sneaky thoughts and immorality had replaced the strength, and the necessity, of the existence of a pure heart and the power of a healthy mind.

But, no matter what, people who wanted to resist would never give up without fighting. True love would never die; true love will always be there for everyone who is eager to discover the needs of his heart without cutting off the desires of his soul which always wants to come up to the surface of life.

Wars, immigration, financial crisis, unemployment and hate had taken over leaving our world exposed in the chaos of uncertainty.

We stopped delivering our dreams in the hands of God and now our future seems like a dry leaf which we left in a devil's hand.

***

"I don't want to lose you! I love you so much, but I can't live like this for the rest of my life."

I froze in fear and tried to remain calm, struggling to pull myself back together because she needed to hear me saying everything would be fine. But I couldn't lie, and I didn't expect I would come across another panic-stricken situation.

"You don't deserve this, we don't deserve this. You are never home and we rarely talk. We failed but we are not the only persons in the world who lost everything. I don't want to leave you, but I can't take it anymore, baby, and I just can't pretend all is well."

I was tired. I had just finished my work and, now, I was in my car listening to my partner as I looked forward to going back home. I could hear the raindrops on the cold glass while I had nothing to say about the way she sounded. Her sweet voice was fighting back sighs. I was sure she was shaking and I wasn't next to her side when all she needed was a hug.

The last months, while trying to offer my partner the best I could, I lacked contact with reality and I hadn't realized that I had managed to make things between us complicated. I thought that working all day for a few bucks and meeting new, difficult challenges, for nothing other than vanity, were serious problems.

I was still shocked as I could hear my partner gasping, guessing she was moving too fast toward her car to avoid the noise of the crazy town, and to find some time to come closer to the truth, trying to remember the past, our past and the way we used to be and act. My girl was striving to remain calm but I knew she wanted to cry. She had no more patience. And, after a while, she took a deep breath and managed to shatter my heart for a second time by being honest.

"I don't want to lose you, baby, but I can't live like this anymore, and this time I mean it. I miss the man I fell for, I miss my man. Please, baby, tell me everything will be fine, let's go back home together."

My mouth ran dry. I could hear my heart pounding in my chest, but still, I found the courage to sound positive and strong.

"Everything will be fine. I promise we will make it so there is no need to worry so much, my love. We will talk about our future and we will decide about our next step. Just be home early," I said, vaguely as I was sure I would never forget that night.

"Okay, I love you."

I was taken aback because I had run into true love but, unfortunately, I hadn't realized that my partner was living a hell. She didn't miss money or success, she never cared about wealth and glory, she wanted to see me smiling again and she missed watching my big eyes in silence while sharing my secret thoughts with her.

We knew each other for more than ten years. We loved spending time together and we were extremely lucky since we had discovered the ideal combination to keep living together while feeling like living the first day life had brought us face-to-face. We were sure that only death would do us part, and we loved teasing one another, thinking about the way our relationship would evolve the next years, the next decades.

For the time being, I felt relieved that my girl was healthy and safe but the thought of losing one another had already crossed my mind and, since that moment, the unwanted thinking didn't stop haunting my soul.

***

The moment we opened the door of our new home in another county we felt weird. We had left our base to set up our small business and, since we had lost our jobs due to the financial crisis and although we believed our new beginning would be successful and we would finally make it, we came across failure after failure. We were wrong and the nasty experience was like fighting against an absurd fate where we could do nothing but hope things would change. We were disappointed; we believed there was something strange in our new place. We thought the whole area was surrounded by negative energy that was focused on us and would never leave us alone. But we had never noticed other people as well, we hadn't seen anyone smiling, having fun.

In a few months, we had lost our savings and we could do nothing to change things. We had never thought that things might have not worked well because we needed to be optimists. Then again we had never thought about the consequences of our decisions.

After the horrible experience, the wall of silence had invaded our life and, as time passed by, the distance between us started getting bigger and bigger. The sweet memories of the past had turned into ash. We were angry. We avoided talking, smiling and even making love. We had become two strangers living under the same roof. In a flash, we had managed to turn our beautiful home into a house where we both felt guilty, and hated it as well.

Life didn't treat us well and, unfortunately, we didn't seek the light in our souls by thinking of our first dinner when we talked all the time about everything. Instead, we became distant; we locked our thoughts in the closet of loneliness, although we could just say, *"Hello! I am here!"*

Fear, stress and agony had enveloped our minds whereas countless, silent questions demanded immediate answers. And then, we discovered that it was easy to say I love you, but it was very difficult to prove it. We had discovered that we ought to make obvious our feelings, revealing our sincere and deeper emotions to overcome the crisis.

Flirting with uncertainty and fighting against difficult situations were conditions that millions of people every day, all around the world had to deal with, and we were not the exception to the rule.

But knowing we were running out of time, we became eager to act as soon as possible. We struggled to change our life; we rushed to reconsider our living and the way we used to see things because we were not willing to surrender a beautiful relationship in the absolute dark.

Considering there were people around us experiencing the other side of life, the ruthless one, I appreciated everything life had given me so far, and felt I was blessed. Yes, I was still a lucky man since I was healthy, and I was still able to understand that my partner had sacrificed her needs to see me getting back from life everything destiny had stolen from us. I had made mistakes but, now, I would do anything to see her beautiful smile again. I realized I was not alone and I would never risk losing my girl.

That night I realized I should be honest and more demonstrative. I decided to speak up because that was not the life I dreamed of, and I was relieved knowing that my partner didn't like it either. All we would have to do was have a beautiful discussion where we would talk about our priorities and goals as a couple and our needs individually. Two simple things combined to make one to save our relationship.

I recalled the moment I heard her trying not to cry a tear and swore to God it would never happen again because I loved her too much to see her suffering. And I missed her big eyes, and her pained smile.

I was anxious and kept waiting for my partner to come back home as I was nervous and couldn't stop moving around the small living room.

While watching the white ceiling and looking forward to hearing her footsteps on the tiled floor, there was still one question dancing in my mind.

"Are we alone in this world?" then again,

"Are we supposed to walk toward the path of life hand in hand? "

"Hand in hand," I thought, and never doubted again.

***

"Hand in hand, my love. I am here, you are not alone in this world," I whispered and smiled, feeling confident again. And, now, I believed I could prove it.

"Hand in hand," she whispered, and I looked into her big eyes where I could see the mirrors of her soul and my reflection on them.

I had found my peace again, I felt like I had gotten past a living nightmare that wanted to ruin everything left while destroying my dreams and my partner's hopes. But, we had just discovered again that we both wanted the same things, we loved spending time together and living under the same roof.

We were delighted because we hadn't lost the game of love and, after that night, we decided to move forward leaving the past behind us. We promised we would never spend our time in vain again. We rushed to fix the problem before it was too late.

The thought of losing one another had never crossed my mind so seriously before because I regarded that, no matter what, I would never leave her side while she would stand by me forever. We knew each other for many years, we shared everything, and we had the delusion that this was enough to make it last until the last day of our life.

But we had forgotten to expose our feelings about life, about our life and that night we did something great. We decided to get past the fears and the presence of the constant insecurity about our future by ignoring all the nasty facts.

That night we decided to focus on us. We talked and laughed like the old days, and we left the nasty place where we had lost our money, ourselves and our time.

We returned back home, back to our base where we found our shelter again, and although things were still difficult, we were happy. We loved talking and we stopped using the word *"love"* in vain.

Le Bal des Abeilles

Chapter One

"I am gonna getcha!" the woman crackled, her hands outstretched like a creepy witch. She followed after the little girl, pretending that she couldn't get closer to her.

"No, you will not!"

Brooke loved spending her time with her niece and it was obvious that she looked forward to playing their favorite game again with Joan. She enjoyed sharing carefree moments with the blonde angel who had stolen her heart, and moreover, it was her only chance to get past her fears and agony.

For the last three weeks, they would run into the house, screaming and trying to avoid one another's attack. The little girl rushed to escape, thinking of her options since she could either go straight under the huge, black table or toward the large, white sofa and hide behind it. The spacious living room was the best place for pillow fights and they both seemed eager to keep on having fun.

Brooke was really happy and looked impatient to getting her life back. She had started making thoughts and plans for the future, considering the possibilities of having her own family, and this time, she was sure she would make it.

The terrifying feeling of flirting intensely with death in her late thirties had vanished, and now she looked forward to living her life again. She was thirty-eight, but she didn't care about her age and the way she would look in the future. She had managed to reconsider the real meaning of life and respect the privilege of coming across the daylight every day that passed by.

"I need a break," Brooke said as she tried to catch her breath.

"Are you okay?" Joan was seven years old and looked like a beautiful doll. Her blonde, curly hair and her big, blue eyes showed off her sweet appearance.

"I am fine, Joan, but I think we should hurry up and fix everything because your mom is going to be here in a few minutes and we have a lot to do." Brooke looked around her and so did Joan.

"I will help you out," Joan whispered.

They rushed to fix the mess while accusing, teasing and laughing at one another for their careless behavior. Brooke was trying to clean the chips and the chocolate from the white carpets as Joan was dealing with the chaos in the kitchen, blaming her aunt for everything.

"Next time we will order Chinese food." Joan intoned as she took a few more steps and knelt, staring at her aunt.

"Are you crazy? Who's going to clean the rice from the carpets?" Brooke answered and looked Joan into her tiny eyeballs, waiting to see her beautiful smile.

"You will clean everything," the girl murmured and Brooke held her hands and locked her niece in her arms, biting softly her neck.

"I love you so much," the skinny woman said.

"I love you too, Brooke." Joan hugged tight her aunt and didn't have the least-intention of letting her go.

"I am glad you didn't call me aunt."

"You are my second mom and I love you so much," Joan whispered while she stretched out her arms to make her aunt see that she would always have her love and hugs. At the same time, a torrent of tears made its appearance on Brooke's pale face, flooding her heart and soul with hope and euphoria.

"You are my precious baby," she said

Her niece looked back at the door. "I think I heard the elevator," Joan exclaimed and stood up.

"Oh no…!" The woman sounded like a little girl too.

"Red alert, mom is here, I repeat, mom is here." They always had a great time together.

"Go to bed and pretend you are sleeping— otherwise your mom will kill us both." Brooke said, smiling at her niece.

***

"How are you?" Mel caressed her sister's back as she stood in front of the large door of the living room.

"I'm fine, Mel." Brooke sounded nervous.

"In a few months, everything will be different." Mel truly believed her words, and loved seeing her sister in her house.

"I know that, Mel." Brooke kept looking outside.

"Then why are you sad?" Mel said angrily.

"I don't like this weather. I miss the sun and the heat!" Brooke said. Mel smiled and hugged her older sister.

Although she knew what could still make her sister worry, she didn't say anything else about her behavior and cheerless mood. They stood at the windows, but both looked impatiently to the coming of summer and the high temperatures as well.

The view from the fifth floor was amazing and they could see everything covered by the snow. The streets, the trees, the cars and the signs were not visible anymore and the countless snowflakes wouldn't stop covering everything.

The severe winter had made everyone stay at home and they were all really angry about that. The majority of the residents of the small town were trapped behind the walls without having the comfort to accomplish all those they wanted and needed to do. Everyone had a bad case of cabin fever.

The last two months, Brooke had had to remain inside the house and avoid getting ill since she needed rest, and of course time to forget the adventure she had experienced. The bad weather didn't help at all.

"Let's talk about the summer holidays." Mel held her sister's hand and then they both headed toward the fireplace.

"What do you mean?" Brooke sounded serious.

"What are your plans for this summer? Mel asked.

"I have no plans," Brooke said vaguely.

"I see." Mel shook her head and smiled.

As usual, they kept talking for the whole night of many things while the snowflakes and the extremely low temperatures carried on turning the whole state into a frozen wasteland.

Chapter Two

Brooke and Mel walked down the streets, making plans for the weekend. The heat and the sun had brought the light and the carefree mood back in their lives, whereas the beautiful roses and the smell of the grass outside the small, white houses helped them dream of the best vacations they had lived, and wait patiently for the next weeks.

The last days of May were amazing since the high temperature during the daylight and the shinning stars during the nights had made everyone's wish come true, pushing everyone into taking the next step, dealing with the preparations for the upcoming summer days. The residents of the small town loved gardening, having their houses neat and painting their old furniture.

The two sisters didn't stop waving at the kind people while asking questions about their plans and projects. One aged couple loved spending their time at home, joking while tidying the garden and painting the huge pots for their new colorful flowers.

When Brooke knelt on the ground and smelled the yellow roses, she rolled her eyes and thought about how lucky she was.

A few meters further, a young couple had decided to clean the small pool and had already placed the big table and the comfortable chairs at their backyard again.

"It's so beautiful!" Brooke said.

"Yes, it is," Mel smiled at her sister and pointed at the house opposite them.

A young boy was playing with his dog while his parents didn't stop looking at their son, feeling happy and proud of their only child.

"Watch out!" Brooke held her sister's hand and dragged her to the sidewalk.

"I'm sorry!" a girl shouted out.

Brooke and Mel stood still, gazing at the children who kept running with their bicycles, showing off their skills in an effort to steal the admiration and the attention of the small neighborhood.

"I love summer!" Brooke said.

"Me too!" Mel was happy for many reasons.

The following weeks, the two sisters along with Joan didn't stop having fun and going out.

Brooke was healthy; she could touch her skin and feel beautiful again since her blonde hair had started making their appearance on her head, while her complexion had become the same as it was used to be, making her an attractive, sweet woman.

The nightmare was gone, she had won the worst enemy of her entire life, and now she felt ready to accept the new challenges that would come up. The following months she would have to abstain from anything stressful and she felt guilty for not helping her sister with their family business. On the other hand, Mel was clear and had warned her sister many times. *"You better stay at home and have fun—otherwise I will close the café and come over there to show you who the boss is."*

Brooke rubbed her eyes and smiled as she waited for her sister and Joan to put on their clothes and go out to watch the fireworks.

***

The beautiful square had everything anyone could imagine since they could see countless local products, books, drinks, and clothes. The traditional local festival of happiness had made everyone celebrate the arrival of summer, while the wind of change had brought the path of calmness closer to their lives.

Brooke looked happier than ever as Mel kept admiring her sister for her spirit and energy. Out of the blue, she grabbed her sister's hand and along with Joan, they started dancing, challenging the rest of the people to do the same thing.

In a few minutes, more than two hundred people were dancing and laughing, forming a chain where the positive energy was able to defeat everything sad and take the ghastly mood away.

"I have a surprise for you," Mel said, dancing with her sister.

"I hate surprises, so tell me now," Brooke said with a little laugh.

"I will not tell you yet," Mel answered seriously.

"Oh, come on, Mel." Brooke looked impatient.

"I will tell you anything you need to know in two days," Mel said, looking away and increasing her sister's curiosity.

"I could bite you like a vampire!" Brooke said. Mel started laughing at her and showing her her teeth.

Chapter Three

"Are you joking?" Brooke was surprised.

"No, I am not." Mel looked into her big eyes and then held her sister's head, touching noses with her.

"Can we afford this?" Brooke asked seriously.

"Listen to me, Brooke. I want you to go there and have fun." Mel was serious too and meant every single word.

"Thank you, Mel." Brooke nodded at her sister and hugged her tight.

"Enjoy your trip!" Mel said as she walked to the door.

"I will!"

"And have sex with someone you like!" Mel shouted as she closed the door behind her, leaving her sister alone, making dreams.

***

The moment Brooke got off the plane and stepped in the airport, she couldn't control her feelings. She started dancing and waving rhythmically at the beautiful women.

Being on vacation in Hawaii has always been her secret desire and now that she was there. She would do anything to have fun and seal the memories in her mind forever.

When she got in the taxi and looked at her watched the beautiful lei and smelled the colorful flowers, she smiled and felt wonderful. She had everything she wanted and looked forward to dancing the hula, the traditional dance of the magic islands.

On her way to the hotel, Brooke was able to see the huge, green mountains, the sun and the peaceful sky. The smell of the coconut trees along with the scent of the suntan oil made her soul rest in paradise. She rolled her eyes and thanked God for saving her life and for giving her the best sister in the world.

"Aloha!" the taxi driver said.

"Aloha!" she whispered as she waved at the polite, middle-aged driver.

Brooke walked toward the reception of the hotel and seemed impatient to change her clothes; she wanted to get rid of the tight white jeans and her white t-shirt. Being in Hawaii meant nothing but fun, swimsuit, sun oil, sunglasses and intense desire to flirt with life.

***

The following hours, Brooke looked completely different and seemed to enjoy herself. Although her skin had turned red, she kept strolling on the white beach and feeling the hot, white sand on her feet, brushing her blonde hair away from her face, happy it was long again. She was as beautiful as she used to be in the past and wasn't willing to waste her time as well.

The black swimsuit showed off her curves while the big, white hat and the silver bracelets on both her wrists and ankles made her look like a celebrity, maybe an actress who needed time to have some rest and leave everything behind.

When she closed her cell phone and thanked her sister yet again, she walked to the hotel, looking around her and thinking of her options and plans for her first night in the island of seduction. She was staying for five days in paradise and she didn't want to miss anything.

The exotic beach-bar near the wooden sidewalk stole her attention and, immediately, Brooke smiled as she already knew what she would do afterwards. She decided to have some rest and come back at the beach later to taste the famous cocktails and maybe to meet the love of her life.

Chapter Four

Brooke took off her white heels and held them with her right hand, impatient to reach the beach-bar and have some fun. The stars and the heat along with the beautiful music triggered her intention to do anything to feel amazing. After an incredible dinner, she wanted to dance, drink and meet new people.

Brooke wore a long colorful skirt and a small white top, leaving her back and her arms uncovered. The pink lipstick, her big, green eyes and her curly hair made her look fabulous, the consummate female who looked for joy, respect and love.

"Brooke!"

The woman turned back and smiled.

"Justin!" Brooke was surprised.

"What are you doing here?" the man asked.

"I was going to ask you the same thing!" Brooke said with a little laugh.

"I decided to thank myself for being a nice man, so I took the plane and came here to have some rest." Justin stared at her and laughed.

"Mel wanted to give me a gift, so I am here because of my sister."

"That's great," Justin said sincerely. He couldn't take his eyes off of her.

"Yea, I think it's great too," Brooke said softly, and smiled.

They walked to the bar and drank the famous cocktails while talking about their lives and childhood. They had known one another since they were children and there was always something between them.

***

The night Brooke along her sister and Joan went to the festival, Mel watched them talking and realized they were meant to be together. They were both acting weird and seemed shy while doing their best to coming up many subjects to keep on talking.

Later that night, Mel approached Justin and learned about his vacations, and didn't lose her time. The following day she arranged everything concerning her sister's trip to Hawaii since she knew what her sister was missing.

Mel was sure that Brooke needed a partner in her life, a serious man to hold her hand and reassure her that everything would be good. And the owner of the small book store was the perfect match for her sister.

Justin was in his early forties, single, handsome, smart and extremely kind with women. And he also seemed to be crazy in love with Brooke, as he was there for her and never stopped asking about her condition when she was fighting for her life. He never gave up on her and didn't move on, although many women liked him and used to flirt with him.

***

"I like your shirt." Brooke said.

"Are you kidding me?" Justin asked while staring at his colorful shirt.

"It looks like my skirt." Brooke smiled and so did he.

"Do you want it?" Justin asked.

"Yea, it would be perfect." Brooke laughed at him while Justin unbuttoned and took off his shirt.

"It's yours." Justin covered her back as Brooke gazed at his body.

"Let's go to the beach," she said.

They spent the rest of the night on the beach talking about their lives, staring at the ocean and sipping their drinks. They loved being there together, but they were both hesitant to make the next step as well.

The flames of the large torches around the beach-bar and along the beachfront added to the romantic tension as the atmosphere started becoming more erotically charged.

"We are in Hawaii and I think I want to do something crazy," Brooke whispered.

"What do you mean?" Justin asked as Brooke looked around her.

"I want to swim naked," Brooke murmured.

"I think it's a great idea," Justin sounded impatient and delighted.

Brooke got up and took off her clothes while Justin watched. When she got into the water, Justin took off his clothes too and followed her in.

The following minutes they came closer and left their bodies and minds free as the moonlight continued enlightening the peaceful surface of the ocean.

Chapter Five

"*Le bal des abeilles...*" Justin whispered.

"What does that mean?" Brooke looked into his big blue eyes and waited for his answer.

They were sitting on a bench, sharing glimpses of love and respect, watching Joan who loved making circles with her bicycle.

When Justin mentioned the dancing of the bees, Brooke smiled at her partner and leaned to his chest. As he held her tight, she thought of his words and tried to hide the tears of happiness and relief.

During the spring, the younger bees along with the new queen leave their nest behind and move on to better places to make a new beginning. When they do that, they start dancing in the air while looking forward to settling into their new home.

Brooke had managed to make a new beginning as well since she had a new partner and was healthy.

***

Immediately after their amazing vacations, Justin and Brooke came back home and shared countless lovely moments and unforgettable nights.

The first days of August were incredible since every night they used to go out and eat ice cream, watch movies at the beautiful open cinema of the small town and do many other simple things that demanded nothing but cheerfulness and interest.

They used to spend their weekends strolling around the lakes and the valleys while caressing the horses of their best friends. Horseback riding was really cool.

Justin knew Brooke loved reading romance novels and every night he used to bring her home the books of her favorite authors. He would never forget the moments they were sitting in the yard drinking lemonade and eating apple pie.

And they would never forget the lovely trip to Hawaii which brought them closer and made them realize that they were meant to be together.

Lullaby

If you really don't mean some words, don't spit them out.
It's easy to say *I love you*, but it's very difficult to prove
it...

A.A Schenna

"Where have you been?" Heidi rushed to hug him. Now that she could see him, she felt like walking on the pink clouds of the most powerful love in the universe.

"Heidi," surprised, the young woman looked into his beautiful eyes and sensed the net of love surrounding their presence, killing all their enemies.

"I am here." David said while trying to make her calm.

Heidi nodded and later leaned on his chest where she untied his leather coat and placed her head on his heart. She needed to listen to his heartbeat to make sure he was fine.

Heidi, in that moment, felt she was the luckiest woman in the world. She had found the best man and he had returned. Her best friend didn't give up on her, the ideal partner, her lover was safe and now kept holding her tight. David was next to her side and he would do anything to stay together forever. He hadn't betrayed her trust and her sensitive heart, although he knew the consequences of his action.

Heidi was now able to think clearly, after many hours she stopped shaking and ran into positive thoughts. Since she could touch his strong body and feel his hot breath on her neck, she was certain they would make it.

Then again, she was curious about her lover's adventure, but she didn't ask any questions. As long as he was there, at their shelter and could touch his cold skin, she was grateful to God.

For more than three hours, David was running like a maniac through the white valley, on the cold snow under the moonlight, while fighting against the soldiers of the King and the bad weather conditions. It was freaking freezing out there, he had lost his horse and he felt that he would collapse. But the desire to find Heidi and leave everything behind was getting stronger and stronger, and he would never surrender.

David had stolen the heart of a beautiful woman, and that was a crime because that woman was supposed to get married to the Prince of Green Valley. The soldiers had invaded his home, grabbed his horse, and everything else he had, and they wouldn't stop unless they would arrest him.

"Hold it, this key belongs to you. David, you are the one who has the right to lock my heart and never let me fall in love again." Heidi stretched out her arm and offered him the golden key while watching her lover silently touching her palm, caressing her thin, cold fingers and then holding tight the key of her heart in his hands.

"I have already given you mine, I belong to you, Heidi and, no matter what, I will never stop thinking of you. I love you and I am not afraid of the King and his soldiers. I am afraid of God and I trust our Lord, and I am sure He will help us get away from here allowing us to live our life in a peaceful place where we will raise our children and will become the happiest couple in the world. Somehow, I believe we will manage to build our home across the waterfalls, watching the snow covering the valley during the cold days and nights of the winter, smelling the flowers and the vineyards during the carefree days of the summer."

"I love you, David."

"I love you too, Heidi."

She hugged him and rolled her eyes thinking about his words, making dreams about their future, feeling proud of the man she had trusted and had decided to live with for the rest of her life.

For once more, Heidi could hear the melody of his heart. She could still hear the most beautiful lullaby, like all the times they used to share the love while becoming one in the small cave, when they lied in front of the fire, touching one another and playing, intensely, the game of love feeling the heat of the fire while ignoring the colorless scene, and the countless dangers of the wild nature along with the starving curiosity of the brutal community.

Heidi was in love with her best friend, David was crazy in love with the nymph of seduction, and they could both listen to the melody of love, the one that only true lovers knew.

For a last time, they were able to listen to the lullaby of love, the sweetest lullaby of all.

***

"Look at the bubbles!" Heidi said, and searched for his sight.

"Yea, it's pretty amazing, there must be millions of them looking for us!" David smiled at her and followed her toward their secret shelter.

Bubble dance, yes, those were the right words to describe the magic phenomenon that used to take place all the time in a beautiful location, in the place where everything started. Their love was born in the most wonderful area of the county. Green Falls was the setting where they first met while following the sound of love.

***

Every winter, on the sunny days, they used to hide under the huge caves holding their hands tightly, making dreams for a better life and hoping their plans would come true, ignoring the complaints, the warnings and the nasty words of their families. They were children; they were living in a country where no one had the right to decide about his own life. They were two kids who would never compromise and would always abstain from becoming slaves.

Heidi and David loved feeling free and they hated adjusting to the reality that the structure of their society used to impose to everyone. They were both raised by farmers and never went to school since their families couldn't pay for their expenses. David and Heidi grew up in the beautiful fields along with the horses and the cows, far away from the cities and the comforts of the modern people of their time.

As time passed by, Heidi turned out to become the most beautiful woman in the small town where the richest and the most powerful men wanted to meet her in order to marry her, while David turned into a good looking farmer and a good man, but remained a poor man who would always come across many obstacles while trying to set up his own home and make his own family. David was a strong man, a clever man who also knew that having strength didn't matter since being physically strong never meant anything except in the ancient years when men had to be strong to evolve, achieve their goals and overcome the challenges.

***

The usual sound of the waterfall, the bubbles that flew around the caves, and the many colorful birds that kept singing the song of love and serenity had already sealed their minds. All they wanted was to come closer; they both looked forward to tasting the flavor of the absolute love, although Heidi was the woman that the King wanted to marry with his own son. She never forgave the first time she saw the King when he announced that he would kill everyone who would dare to insult his daughter-in-law. Nevertheless, Heidi decided to listen to her heart and she would never betray her soul since David was, and would always remain, the man she wanted.

Heidi and David would dare to become a couple regardless of the traditions, the reaction and the fears of their parents, and no matter what the others would say. They didn't care about the local community and the fact that everyone would be ready to judge them for their right to be together and share the love the way they wanted.

"Are you sure you want this, Heidi?" David asked.

"Yes, David." Heidi kissed his lips as the young man pulled her blonde hair back and caressed softly her face.

"I am just a farmer," David said, and Heidi placed her hands on his red cheeks.

"Do you love me?" Heidi asked him, and sounded like a little girl who felt the need to sound like a serious, adult woman.

"Yes, I do, Heidi," the golden-haired man said.

"I love you too, David. I would do anything to spend the rest of my life with you."

Now Heidi placed her hands around his waist and tried to make his blue eyes focus on hers, getting the assurance he was searching for.

The following minutes they did what they always wanted. They were making love in front of the fire as the dark had already covered the county and the snow was getting ready to put on another dress, with a different color, a red color.

David and Heidi felt safe in the cave, they seemed happy sharing the most incredible emotions. They both felt like flying in the air, and no one was able to steal their moments from their memories, not even death.

"I heard something," Heidi whispered, and looked into his eyes.

"Don't you dare cry a tear for me," David said, and she nodded.

Heidi was able to hear the melody of his heart again; David could feel her heartbeat on his chest. They were lucky, they were true lovers, and they could hear the melody of their hearts. They could listen to the lullaby of love…

Limitless Love Collection

Silent Love…

Chapter One

As always, Celina looked fabulous and didn't stop smiling, while sharing her joy with her guests. She kept walking around, talking with her friends, and stealing everyone's attention.

I had heard that some people have charisma, an ability to make someone feel special, and Celina was that kind of person. She was talented in making other people feel nice and to disregard their worries. As long as you could stare at her big eyes, and listened to her sweet voice, you could get past everything sad and, additionally, you had the chance to reconsider your way of life. Then, you would either become eager to focus your mind on all those that could make you really happy, and try to understand them, or you would try to make a new beginning, remaking your likes and priorities, ignoring the past and the nasty facts.

I would say that I was sure about my view since I had the privilege to know Celina many years and she always had a unique way to affect my life. I would never forget the times she used to support my decisions about school, studies and, unfortunately, candidate girlfriends. I had attempted many times to make her feel jealous, but in vain.

Every time I looked at her sweet face, I could still remember the second time I tried to tell Celina that I would remain in love with her forever.

We were not children. We were seventeen and we loved walking while looking up at the sky and counting stars. The summer night was incredible; the smell of the sea, and Celina's perfume, had seduced my mind and all I wanted was to spend the rest of my life with my princess.

The moment I was ready to reveal my secret, Celina raised her hand and sealed my lips. When I saw the teardrops running down her cheeks, I felt terrible because I had managed to shatter her heart for a second time. My beautiful princess was shaking as I rushed to hide the ring; I was ready to show her, in my pants. I had given all my money from my savings to surprise her, but I still couldn't find the way to see her smiling. I could do nothing to help her overcome the painful experience she had lived, because of me. I would give my life to change things and get the Celina I knew back.

Her gaze had made my heartbeat run faster than the speed of light and, at that moment, all I wanted was to hold her tight in my hug and never let her go.

Celina hoped I would forget her and waited to see me falling in love with another girl but, finally, she realized that she would have to kill me in order to get her out of my mind.

Yes, she needed time to pull herself back together and adjust to reality, but I was crazy in love with her and I remained selfish. I also looked forward to having her back in my life ignoring her priorities.

I used to fight with everyone, and argue with my family since I never read anything for the school, and I did all those things because I couldn't stop thinking of Celina.

My princess would hate seeing me trapped in the zone of pretentiousness. That was the only reason she used to be distant and abstained from coming closer to me. Nevertheless, she never liked seeing me miserable or having the facial expression of a guilty man. Celina had told me many times that I owed her nothing.

Now, the party was great and we all had great moods. We loved drinking beers and dancing under the moonlight as we also liked flirting with optimism and joy.

"It's a great party," the girls said, while John smiled at her.

"Thanks, guys," Celina caressed her brother's back and looked toward me.

The moment I saw her dark eyes, I recalled the time we were strolling at the beach, hand in hand, fully in love. I could still remember her expression when I had told her that one day we would get married and have many children. She had locked her eyes on me and she had shaken her head yes, while I was determined to make that happen.

Celina couldn't stop kissing me and holding me tight whereas she kept telling me that she would do anything for me. Unfortunately, a week later, she proved the meaning of her words.

I came back to reality and watched Celina talking with the girls. The way she had looked at me a couple of minutes earlier had triggered my will, as the secret desires, the limitless passion and my love for Celina had already enveloped my thoughts.

That night everything was so beautiful and all I really missed was having my princess in my arms, staring at her sweet face and stealing her kisses again.

"Are you okay?" John asked.

I nodded at him, but I was lying and he was able to realize my terrible reaction. To be honest, I felt horrible because John was one of my best friends, but I also knew that I had to do something to reassure my girl that I would always stand by her side. I would risk losing my best friend to get her back.

Now, either I would confess my feelings in front of everyone and accept her final rejection, or I would try to forget her forever.

"I'm fine, John," I whispered.

I walked toward the mini bar and I realized that my presence didn't drop her sight. My princess followed me back and, after a while, she came to my side.

In a flash, I remembered the time I had a party at my house and she kept her eye on me because she believed I was drinking beers when I shouldn't. That, and because she believed alcohol would kill me. She always wanted to protect me, as the only thing I was impatient to do was having her in my hug and telling her how much I loved her.

But, what am I saying...? It was not just love, Celina was my obsession, the most wonderful addiction in my microcosm, and she had remained the most significant part of my life's dream.

The moment Celina stood in front of me I could hardly breathe and move. My eyes locked on hers as I waited to hear her sweet voice.

"Hi, Brandon, how are you?" Celina was divine.

I left my drink on the bar while trying to pull myself back together. I was confused. I was despaired while I was thinking that she had no right to decide for both of us and, moreover, she had no right to choose the best option for my future, according to her view, ignoring that I was the only one who could actually do that.

"I love you," I said.

As expected, Celina was taken aback. She was polite and smiled at me and, after a while, she left my side without saying a word.

I continued looking at her until her brother, John, my best friend, came closer to me and tried to find out what I intended to do. Meanwhile, I didn't stop watching her dark eyes and her long, black hair.

"Is everything okay?" John asked.

"I'm in love with your sister," John rolled his eyes and placed his left hand on my shoulder.

"Why don't you leave her alone?" John wanted to warn me, but I didn't care.

"I love her," I would risk losing my best friend.
***

The following morning we all met at the beach. We enjoyed spending Sunday mornings near the sea as we used to walk and drink coffee while staring at the huge waves.

We were six people wondering about everything and we never stopped making dreams and plans for the future.

Celina was also there and, initially, she was acting weird, like a stranger, but not for too long. For once more, and while still being at the small café, she had managed to show her interest about me by rushing toward my side. I was ready to fall off my seat but, in no time, Celina had gotten up from her chair and had already grabbed my arm.

I was not naïve, careless or stupid but, sometimes, I served as a magnet attracting the strangest facts and things without being able to explain the cause.

Later, Celina avoided looking at me and I hated seeing her acting like that. I had screwed up everything, I had caused her a lot of pain, and countless questions about our relationship, our future and, for a moment, her behavior made me think that I shouldn't be there. I felt like I didn't belong in the company of my best friends.

I knew I had destroyed our connection but I was twenty-two, crazy in love with Celina and panicked as well since I was ready to ask my princess to marry me.

I would never say that I was a great catch but I had finished my studies, I had my own small business with candies and I earned a lot of money. And above all, I could swear that every day, I would do my best to make my princess happy.

Celina carried on ignoring my presence until the moment I stood up when, out of the blue, she glanced at me and, after a while, I heard her sweet voice.

"Let's take a walk," Celina gazed at me and sounded sweet, but serious as well.

"Okay," I said.

We left the small café while our best friends were still hooked by her reaction and the way she looked at me.

***

"Do you remember?" she asked.

When Celina pointed at the huge rocks in the sea, the memories of the terrible accident and the worst moments of my life came up.

I held her hand and I was sure she could feel my heartbeat. Although I felt wonderful touching her, like the times I used to pick her up from her home to go out and have fun, I couldn't stop feeling responsible for the worst experience she had ever lived.

If only I could turn back the time and had the ability to change things. I would rather die and see her happy from somewhere up there, than suffering because of me.

"Yes, I do," I said.

"Are you sure that you love me? Do you think I'm still beautiful?" Celina was ready to cry.

"Are you serious?" I asked.

"Of course, I'm serious," Celina took off her white dress and I gazed at her body.

Although she wore a black swimsuit that made her look gorgeous, I couldn't pretend that everything on her body was perfect. But I believed she was incredible since my eyes could see the beauty of her heart and the wealth of her soul.

Then again, Celina regarded that I should face up the truth and adjust to reality. Nevertheless, she acted this way to help me step back, sacrificing her own happiness and future. She would hate seeing me emotionally trapped and feeling sorry for her.

Yes, the scars were still there and her skin would never be as beautiful as it used to be. The signs of the surgeries, the scars around her chest and her belly would remain on her skin forever. The signature of her flirt with the death would be marked on her body for the rest of her life, but I didn't care.

I have been in love with Celina since I was a teenager and I remained in love with a woman who was interested in having a serious relationship, investing on deeper emotions.

As time passed by, her patience, along with her exciting energy, had healed the pain in her soul. Celina had overcome the most difficult part and didn't suffer anymore.

The physical pain was gone but, now, she had to take care of her heart and get rid of her insecurities. She had to trust me.

"No matter what you say, or think, I find you beautiful and yes, Celina, I do love you."

"You don't have to love me, Brandon," Celina said.

"I love you and not because I have to," I answered.

"I will never be able to become a mother. You will never be able to have children with me, Brandon."

Celina held my hands and sounded sweet and honest. She always cared about the others and not for herself.

I placed my hands on her face and caressed her cheeks while, the moment I touched her lips, the teardrops started running down her pale skin.

"I just want to be with you," when my eyes pierced hers, I kissed her lips and I was sure that we would spend the rest of our lives together.

Finally, Celina realized that I had surrendered my life and my soul in her hands and she could do whatever she liked with my heart forever. She had trusted my words and she had accepted my confession.

"I never regretted for saving your life," Celina whispered.

"I know," I rolled my eyes and, for a last time, the worst memories of the past haunted my mind.

If Celina hadn't pushed me away, the Jet Ski would have killed me. Celina had saved my life by offering hers. But God didn't take her and I'm grateful for having her in my life. I could still see and admire my beautiful princess.

"And I never stopped loving you," she murmured.

I locked Celina in my hug.

"I will always love you," I was determined not to let her down, and I never did.

Rebirth…

Chapter Two

"As long as we are strong, everything will get better. I am sure things will change. Have faith my love, try not to give up," I could still remember her words and, for a moment, I felt my heart bleeding.

***

I walked down the street while I kept thinking of our future. As much as we had tried, we could do nothing to change things and retain our hopes. In a few months, we had managed to lose everything we had struggled to achieve.

I never liked being a loser but I also knew the sooner I would accept the freaking situation, the faster I would get out of this chaotic position.

I needed to get past the nasty facts and get everything out of my mind immediately, so I stopped near the huge rocks on the edge of the hill to catch my breath because I felt like drowning in the ocean of depression.

I stared toward the countless, beautiful lights as the puny air, along with the heat, made my spirit eager to fly above the city of angels, pushing me to dare making a new beginning. Although the dark had wrapped up my whole world, the shining stars looked incredible, spreading their glow to despaired souls like mine.

"I love this place," I murmured. The view was really amazing.

I looked behind me and the presence of the large, coconut trees across my sight stole my attention and made me think of the past. I could still remember the first days at Green Hill in California.

I had recovered from the heart attack and I was told by everyone to be careful. My beautiful wife had decided to abandon her dreams to take care of me and see me healthy and strong as usual.

My partner always dreamed of being a successful actress and I was sure she would achieve her goal, but she could never betray her heart since she loved me and, with no doubt, I was definitely the luckiest man on earth. I would never forget her sacrifices, her loyalty to me and her limitless love.

Samantha was talented and I knew that success, independency, and a great career meant everything to her, until the moment we met in New York.

People usually call it love at first sight; I would call it earthquake at first sight since her gaze had managed to shatter my world, my mind, and my soul as I was seeking, almost begging for her attention.

Before our first meeting, I thought I would never get married since I liked being single and having fun all the time, but she was special and I didn't want to lose her. Samantha was exceptional, she was a real lady and I would do anything to see her happy. And I did it. I risked my career and we both lost our futures.

Now, we had no money and, moreover, we would have to sell our house and forget the luxurious way of life. But I never regretted getting married and sharing my life with Samantha. I would never lie to anyone about this and I could cross my heart to convince everyone who could say the opposite.

I was a professional producer and my effort to make a successful movie with my promising, aspiring actress, meaning my wife, came across failure after failure. I had denied working with a diva, a very famous actress and, out of the blue, the system kicked me out of almost all the big studios of Los Angeles. Soon, I found out that all the doors were closed. We had lost everything, but at least we had one another.

I remained silent and kept wondering about our life in another state. I was living the worst period of my life. *"How was I supposed to go back?"* I questioned myself and, although I couldn't find any answer, my mind persisted. *"How was I supposed to go back?"*

I stretched out my arms and, after a while, I felt her hands in the pockets of my bright, blue pants. She knew I loved strolling around the beautiful neighborhood and since I was late, she wanted to make sure that everything was okay.

"What did we do to deserve this?" I murmured.

"It's called bad estimation, but we will make it," I said. Every time I needed someone to support me, Samantha was there.

I turned back and I could see her standing in front of me, spreading her optimism, and showing me her pained smile.

My lovely partner hid in my hug and, then, she held my hands while trying to make me move my legs to dance with her under the moonlight, forgetting our worries.

"There is no music," I whispered.

"I can hear your heartbeat, can't you hear mine?" she said.

Whenever I felt ready to give up, Samantha was there for me. I had screwed up our life. I had destroyed her dreams. I had destroyed my career and my future, but she didn't leave my side nor did she ever intend to dump me.

"I will never leave you, John, you are my man, and you are also my handsome husband," my wife whispered.

"I am so lucky," I murmured while caressing her back.

"As long as you love me…," Samantha hugged me tight as I looked up at the sky.

My wife had managed to blanket my soul with her optimism and, that moment, I felt ready to leave all the nasty facts behind and move on.

Samantha was the best person I had ever met and I was lucky enough to earn her trust and love. We fought very hard against fate but we were both determined to protect our love by any means, keeping away anything that could threaten her survival.

"I will always love you," I smelled her long, blonde hair, rolled my eyes and realized that I had come back to reality.

***

Ten years were enough to turn a beautiful house in the countryside into ruins. All this time, the wonderful Victorian house remained closed and that house was the only property we had. It was our precious shelter, our last place to accommodate our dreams.

"We will make it," Samantha said, but I wasn't sure about that since the house was empty, cold and, without doubt, we needed a lot of money to fix all the damages.

Samantha glanced at me and smiled. She was trying to be cool, but I was sure that she was looking for my support since nothing was going to be easy. We were not in college anymore and, moreover, Minnesota couldn't be compared with New York. We had to change everything and, of course, our way of life.

For once more, my wife had decided to stand by my side, ignoring her needs, her dreams, and desires. Although she could leave me to move on with her life and chase her luck to the industry, Samantha chose to follow my plan and kept sharing her life with me, a husband who had gotten used to letting her down.

But I never gave up trying to make her feel proud of me and reassuring her instincts about her choice.

"In your late thirties it's difficult to make a new beginning," I thought, but I never confessed my opinion to my wife.

Instead, I got rid of the insecurities and became stubborn again. At the time, Samantha was the personification of motivation along with determination and counted on me, I regarded that I had no right to betray her trust. I ought to make it work and, since we had no other option, I had to strive to change everything.

"Of course we will make it," I sounded confident and I could still see that she believed in me.

***

In less than three months, we had a new home. Our farm was the best achievement we had ever come across. There were no words to describe the moment I tasted the honey of our bees trough my wife's lips. I could still remember the taste of perfection and the glow in Samantha's eyes.

"Are you happy?" Samantha asked.

"What?" I was surprised.

"You were a successful producer and look at us now," My wife said.

"I am very happy. Are you happy?" I asked and she nodded at me.

I smiled and then Samantha came closer.

My wife leaned on my chest, placed her fingers on my belly, and started making circles on my blue shirt, while I carried on thinking of her question. *Yes, I was very happy since the fame, the money and the extremely, sexy nights I had experienced could offer you nothing other but vanity.*

We were sitting on the grass, under the shadow of the large pine tree, while the intoxicating smells of the nature fought against the seductive thoughts of the past and were doing their best to make us feel lost in paradise.

When I looked around me, I ran into the zone of the truth and real happiness. I loved the color of serenity while

I also adored her eyes, the leaves of the poplar trees and the surface of the lake in the middle of our farm. Everything was green and I could feel the blossom of nature affecting my whole existence.

Then again, the sound of the colorful birds was incredible. The entire scene was magic and, yes, I was really, really happy because I was located in paradise, holding my lovely wife.

I had the support of a woman who had dared to leave all the comforts she used to enjoy behind her and, now, she dealt with nature while helping me do all the hard work that our farm demanded. I was the luckiest man on earth.

"I am pregnant," she said while I couldn't swallow.

"Take it easy, that's okay now, you can breathe," Samantha laughed and put her fingers on my jaw.

I was living the best moments of my entire life.

***

As days passed by, I realized that, no matter how hard you work, you can't fight destiny. Unfortunately, our achievement was gone, our small business was over and our bees along with our equipment were stolen. In a flash, our dreams vanished and the despair decided to settle in our life again. And, soon, we would run out of money.

I felt I was cursed, but my wife was pregnant and I had no right to let her down. I had to be strong for both of us and I needed to see her believing in me to overcome the obstacles which kept hiding us the road to success and harmony.

"Would you like something to drink?" I asked.

"I am fine, John," Samantha held my hand and waited to see me smiling.

"I love you," I said, and kissed her lips.

"I love you too."

We laid in our bed and continued talking about our baby while teasing one another. In two months he would be with us, and we looked forward to staring and smiling at him.

"What is this smell?" Samantha asked.

"I have no idea," I said vaguely.

"It smells like smoke," My wife said.

The fire had already burned the mountain opposite our farm and, as it seemed, it would destroy everything. Unfortunately, our predictions were true since, in a few minutes, the flames wrapped the beautiful valley and burned everything. There was nothing we could do but abandon our house and our dreams.

Despite the destruction, and the loss of everything we had, I could still see her smile. Samantha was covered by the ash and kept offering her positive energy to me.

"You never gave up on me; you are still here while you could be a successful actress in Hollywood," I said.

"I don't care, I love you," she said and that's all I wanted to hear to make a new beginning again. I guessed I had to get used to flirting with failure after failure.

***

"It's my party…"

When I heard Samantha singing, I laughed and went closer to her side. My wife was holding our son in her hands. Oh gosh, she was so beautiful.

Our baby looked like an angel. He had my hair, my eyes and his mother's nose.

"Black hair, dark eyes and a beautiful nose, at least he took something from me," his mother said with a little laugh.

Samantha stood in front of me and softly bit my lips.

"I love you so much, both of you," Samantha intoned.

"Did you hear what mom said?" It was my turn to take our baby in my hands.

Samantha raised her eyebrows and placed her hands on her hips waiting to see me singing. When I opened my mouth, she laughed at me. She would never stop teasing me.

Fortunately, things had changed and the bad luck had stopped chasing us. We had managed to retain our faith, regardless of the dark paths fate had put us in, and we never stopped hoping for the best.

The birth of our son had made both of us experience the rebirth of our life.

"As long as you love me, baby," Samantha was the personification of love, indeed.

The Key

Chapter Three

"You hold the key."

I had no words to describe the way I felt. The moment my feet sensed the cold water of the ocean, I was sure my heart left my body and flew above the white clouds of euphoria. Then, I looked behind me and they were all sitting on the sand, staring at me.

I could see the beautiful, large eucalyptus while, at the same time, the hot wind didn't stop stealing its wonderful smell and spreading it all over the place.

My wife along with our two little boys looked forward to seeing me joining their company, while John and Leonard were hooked on Amanda's legs making her life difficult. As she was trying to put their funny, blue hats on their heads, I kept smiling while asking myself the reason I had betrayed her trust.

I had met Amanda at the airport in Los Angeles and we both headed to New York. During the flight, I discovered that she was the most interesting woman I had ever talked to and I was impatient to know everything about her.

Amanda was a successful publisher; she loved books and everything concerning the publishing industry. She was thirty-five years old, at that time, and she had never thought the idea of getting married and having children. When we came closer and discovered that we loved the same things, without any further delay, we rushed to get married and have a baby.

Before long, Amanda decided to leave her job, while I was happy that she wanted to focus her attention on the needs of our family, ignoring her satisfaction and desire. The love for the books and the industry had been replaced by the presence of me and our two boys.

Everything seemed perfect and I assumed we had all that we needed until I made the biggest mistake of my entire life and I destroyed our family. I had betrayed everything she had made me promise and she had seen the betrayal in my eyes. I had cheated on her and, the moment I realized what I had done, I was sure I would never overcome my most stupid action ever.

I hated being single and I didn't like one night stands, but no one will ever be perfect.

Now, my beautiful partner waved at me and sent me the love of her heart through a flying kiss.

The entire situation remained weird since the last time I saw my wife she was crying but, this time, Amanda looked happy with no teardrops, no screams and no disappointment. I couldn't explain what was happening.

I took a deep breath, rolled my eyes and laughed because I believed everything was the same as usual. We all liked having fun.

When I sensed Amanda's fingers on my wet skin, the cold water had already covered my body. I continued searching for her eyes, but I couldn't find her.

"You hold the key," Amanda intoned, while I thought it was a kind of game.

I was still able to hear her voice, but I couldn't see her and I didn't stop wondering about that. It was weird while, out of the blue, I recalled the moment she took the babies and left our house. I had confessed to my sin and she was angry at me. I would never forget her facial expression the moment she told me that she wanted divorce.

I was still confused since I could hear her voice, but my mind was locked on the time where I had shattered her heart. *"How could this be possible?"* I kept asking myself.

Suddenly, I opened my eyes and felt I was lost as I was stranded in a beautiful place where I had never been before.

Max, my dog, joined me and rested on the grass while he carried on chewing my white shoes. The last two days, my Canadian white shepherd and my best friend, was acting weird and, although I was standing next to him, I couldn't find any explanation for his behavior. For once more, I called for him to stop but it seemed that Max couldn't hear me.

After a while my best friend disappeared whereas I was left alone in an olive farm gazing upon the bees which flew around the olive trees, the white and the purple thymes, flirting with their precious juices. I could hear the magic sound of their wings and I was ready to fall asleep.

"You hold the key."

I saw Amanda coming closer to my side as she continued whispering the same words, and I still couldn't understand what she meant. But, she looked happy again and she continued smiling at me.

Soon, my eyes focused on her thin fingers and, specifically, on her hands. Amanda held a beautiful, white rose in her hands.

I knelt and locked some purple flowers in my hands because I wanted to offer her something as beautiful as her.

"You are so beautiful, Amanda."

"So are you, Mike."

Amanda wore a long, white dress and looked like a goddess. Then again, her black hair was caught in a beautiful pony tail while her lips had the same color with that one of the passion. I would give everything I had to taste the flavor of her fabulous, red lips.

Although we were both in our early forties, I could bet that her beauty would never fade. *"Oh gosh, why did I cheat on her? My wife is the most beautiful woman in the world,"* I thought.

"Come with me."

Amanda gave me the white rose and took the purple flowers from my sweaty palm. She threw them away and, then, she held my hands.

I was confused, I had no idea what was happening, but I would never forget her smile. I really, really wished she had forgiven my mistake.

"If only you knew how much I missed your big, brown eyes and your curly hair," Amanda whispered.

I looked around me and my wife, along with John and Leonard, were there. I couldn't move and I was still shocked, but I was able to realize that everything I wanted was in that room.

"You hold the key," Amanda's lips touched mine and I heard my little boys laughing.

***

My kids enjoyed my reading them aloud their favorite tales, while I loved seeing them being hooked by the stories their mother had picked up for them.

"Dinner is ready," my wife was lost in the kitchen preparing the food.

Although I had recovered, I could still feel my wife's agony and fear.

When she took our babies and left our house, I collapsed. And I was extremely lucky because Amanda came back home and saved my life. She had forgotten John's favorite game and she couldn't stand his crying.

The moment she opened the door and saw me lying on the white tile floor, she froze in fear. I had fainted and she could do nothing to wake me up.

In one day, I had managed to turn my wife's life into her worst living nightmare. Amanda was scared to death and didn't care about her sacrifices, her career and future but for my life.

***

"Soon, I will leave the house and I will not cause you any problem," I said.

"You don't have to leave," Amanda whispered.

"Are you sure?"

"Yes."

The teardrops kept running down our faces. My wife had abandoned her dreams and her professional life to make me happy and, unfortunately, at some point, I had passed over her sacrifices. I had regretted my faults. I had regretted cheating on her and I would never do it again. I should be grateful; I had the best partner in the world.

That moment we laid in the bed and made love, I was the happiest man on earth since I could still feel her heartbeat on my chest.

Amanda gave me back the key I had lost and, moreover, she was the reason I was still alive. I fought against the danger of losing my family and I would never risk doing the same mistake again.

"Don't forget three words: love, respect, appreciate." Amanda intoned and she was right.

On the Sixth Floor

Chapter One

When Jenna came through the outer doors of her apartment building and stared at her belongings on the sidewalk, the midday sun beating hot on her bare neck and shoulders, she stared at her stuff, helpless. There was no way to do everything in one day, but she never listened to her best friend. She placed her hands on her hips and bit her lips. There were still many huge boxes on the street and she had to rush to take her things up, to her new apartment.

The moment she looked upon her cramped apartment on the sixth floor, she shook her head and seemed ready to give up. *"How am I going to do this?"* She wondered.

Jenna had lost her courage. She missed the hugs and kisses, even though her ex was scum, right now he was the better choice instead of being alone. She had the absurd belief that she was fighting fate for her happiness. And that no matter how hard she tried, she would fail.

And it was obvious that she was exhausted. Seven trips in and out of the building, carrying her precious items were enough to steal her energy. Meanwhile, the sun's rays and the unexpected heat insisted on making her life more difficult. The sweat kept running down her face while she needed something to drink.

Although Jenna believed that it would be easy to move on to better and more interesting experiences while dealing seriously with her personal needs and with her life ignoring the nasty past, she couldn't stop thinking about her future and the decisions she had made. When she rolled her eyes and recalled the strangest facts from her entire life, she changed her mind and stopped having doubts about how her decisions would affect her living in the future.

She pulled her black hair away from her face and rushed to fix the mess starting with the plastic bags and then with the huge boxes. After a while, she took a deep breath, glanced upon her favorite paintings and smiled.

Jenna was flirting with various emotions as her material world looked like a huge mountain ready to fall apart. She looked behind her and waved at the children who watched in silence and waited for her next move. But, regardless of the hard day and the difficulties she had come across, Jenna hadn't regretted her decision to sell her house and move to a new place. It was her chance to live her life the way she wanted and she didn't have the least of intention of stepping back.

It was an unusual and weird day as well (since the new beginning had made her insecurities come up), but the worst experience of her life was over and she was thrilled. Nothing could scare her, not anymore.

Jenna seemed to enjoy the first day at her new neighborhood. After two hours of hard work she decided to take a break and she sat in her favorite chair, staring at the children and the pedestrians who glanced at her curiously.

"I will make it." She loved saying to those who wanted to speak up, but didn't have the courage to open their mouths and talk. Jenna didn't actually care about what people would think because she was fine with herself.

"Good luck." Some teenagers said as she was checking out her emails using her cell phone.

"Thanks!"

Jenna started laughing. She had managed to get away from George, and now that her daily nightmare had vanished, she was single and free to live her life without her liar husband.

The nasty memory made her dark eyes focus on something else and the colorful café stole her attention immediately. The smell of the donuts was amazing and she couldn't resist the guilty desire.

She didn't waste her time; since she needed a coffee and a donut, Jenna left everything behind and ran toward the small café. The last days she was determined to change. Jenna had been a lonely woman, and upon leaving George had decided to do everything she liked. She missed following her heart and acting impulsively.

Before long, Jenna came back and seemed to have fun as for the first time after many years, she felt really happy. She had forgotten the moment she had moved to New York City when she used to do everything depending exclusively on her powers.

Jenna looked confident as positive thoughts flooded her heart and spirit. She had taken the risk to come closer to her happiness and she was also sure that soon, she would smile again.

Jenna had fought very hard to make this happen and being optimistic was the only way to keep on walking toward the road to love. She believed everything would get better, and soon she would be able to go out and meet new people or a new love.

"I think you need someone to help you out with that." The grey-haired man said while pointing at the huge box which was full of clothes and bags.

Surprised at his offer to help, Jenna didn't know how to answer.

"Yes, I guess…" Jenna shook her head and smiled at the handsome stranger.

"My name is John; I live on the sixth floor. I guess you are my new neighbor." The tall man walked to her side and stood in front of her. He offered his hand and waited.

"Nice to meet you, John, I'm Jenna." Jenna cautiously shook John's outstretched hand.

"Glad to meet you, Jenna." His blue eyes locked on hers.

"Thanks, me too," Jenna whispered.

John took the huge box and headed to the stairs as Jenna stood up from her favorite chair, wondering about his attitude. He was kind and she was not used to coming across good guys.

***

After three hours, Jenna was able to see all the huge boxes and the rest of her precious items in her small apartment. John had done a great job and she knew that without his help, she would probably still be out there brushing the dust from her black pants, sweeping the sweat from her forehead while staring at the pile of boxes wondering where to begin.

"Thank you so much, John," Jenna said.

"You're welcome. If you need anything, you will find me here." John pointed at the white door opposite her apartment and smiled at his beautiful neighbor.

"Okay," she whispered.

The following minutes they were both acting weird. Jenna remained stable admiring his body while John looked impatient to hear her beautiful voice again.

"Take care," John said and walked to his apartment.

"Thanks, you too…" His muscles and his beautiful smile had stolen her attention and she couldn't take her eyes off him. He looked pretty good for his age.

When Jenna closed the door behind her, she leaned against the yellow wall and laughed. She had finally made it. She had a home, her own, private shelter.

Although the first glance upon the remaining material past and the mess made her want to cry, she had achieved something great. She had managed to get past the connection to her ex and her previous way of life. But she had to fix the chaos in front of her, which still looked like a rough mountain.

She had to do everything on her own, but she didn't care. It was not going to be easy, but she preferred being optimistic rather than running into the zone of vanity. She had chosen to dare and she had taken the first step to change her living. She had managed to get her life back.

Tears of happiness started running down her face as she breathed in air of relief. Jenna felt she was free. She walked around the small living room and it looked wonderful. She checked out the rest of the rooms of her apartment and began making dreams and plans for the future.

In less than a month, Jenna had gotten rid of a terrible husband who had destroyed her life, and she had found a new place to make a new beginning.

George, her ex-husband, had dumped her for another woman. He cheated on her, didn't care about her feelings. Loyalty meant nothing to him.

Then again, Jenna always had the strength to forget his mistakes and she was also able to find the courage to ignore his behavior and keep living with her husband although, deeply inside her soul, she was sure he deserved nothing. She should have shown no mercy.

Jenna forgave him for everything he did to her, which she now knew was her biggest mistake, although he never felt guilty for his attitude. George had never appreciated her sacrifices to save their marriage and he had never respected the time and her efforts to comply with his weakness and his absurd demands.

But it was not only his fault. They were both responsible for what was happening between them. Jenna walked to the small window of the living room and got rid of the bracelet her ex had offered her during their second date. When she threw it away, she laughed and felt relieved. There were no teardrops; she would never feel guilty again.

***

When they first met, George told Jenna that he wanted to spend the rest of his life gazing at her big brown eyes. But she hadn't realized what an excellent liar. Why he hadn't hesitated to flirt even with her best friend, denying everything of course.

The moment George told Jenna that he was crazy in love with his secretary, she was ready to collapse. George had announced he wanted to marry his mistress since she was pregnant with his child.

Jenna felt the need to delete chapter George from her life and change everything forever. She was determined to laugh, to feel proud of herself, to chase her dreams, to stop flirting with depression, to move on, following her heart and instincts.

Jenna was independent, in her mid-thirties, who loved going out with friends and liked sharing her thoughts with interesting people. Even though she was not a super model, men had a hard time ignoring her presence. She was tall, had a fabulous body and a face that men usually misunderstood. Sometimes, men regarded her pained smile as a promising sign for something wild.

The moment she stepped into her new apartment, she found the light in her soul. She got her life back and she couldn't stand not celebrating the new chapter in her life.

Carla, her best friend, a nurse, like herself, would do everything to see her smiling again and she would always stand by her. They were like sisters and, as expected, they would go out together.

***

"I want you to tell me everything." They liked dancing and drinking but, now, Carla wanted to know more about Jenna's new neighbor and her new experiences.

"There's nothing to tell!" Jenna was nervous.

"Is he single?" Carla asked.

"I have no idea." Jenna blushed as she smiled to avoid Carla's assumptions.

"Why didn't you ask him? Did you see a ring?" Carla was furious. She wanted to help Jenna find her way back to life and happiness.

"I didn't think I should ask him!"

Jenna ordered another drink. Carla stared at her best friend. She pulled her blonde hair away from her face and her dark eyes made her look like a femme fatale. Yes, her best friend would be fine.

Jenna thought Carla was fabulous. She was tall and she had a great body too. And she was crazy in love with her husband. She was a special lady and a good wife.

"What's his name?"

"His name is John."

"What is he doing? How old is he?" Carla was curious, she didn't stop asking questions.

"I have no idea." Jenna smiled. She was sure that Carla wouldn't stop questioning her, whereas she already regretted speaking up.

Jenna looked around and remembered the first time they discovered their favorite bar. Five years had already passed and she was single again without having somebody to love. Jenna wondered about the future, the possibility of getting married for a second time and having children with a special man. If only she could make the time go by slowly.

"What are you waiting for?" Carla sounded serious.

"Are you insane?" Jenna would never dare to make the first step to approach a man.

"Tomorrow you will thank him for his help and then you will be able to ask him everything you need to know." Carla was serious.

"You are insane." Jenna was worried; she didn't think she remembered how to thought that she couldn't flirt with a man.

"Yes, I'm insane." Carla grabbed Jenna's hand and they started dancing.

It was the best day of her life.

Jenna was happy.

Chapter Two

After work, Jenna loved strolling in the park. The towering trees, the smell of the wet grass, the beautiful lake, the colorful flowers, and the countless birds made her feel wonderful. She liked singing her favorite songs as she was looking out at the city and she felt free.

Although Jenna grew up in Georgia, New York was always her favorite city. Now, she regarded the sleepless city her home.

She put on her grey jacket and walked toward her apartment building. The dark had blanketed the city, and pretty soon, the shinning stars would start making their presence in the sky. Their glow would easily steal her attention.

The first week of April reminded her the cold days of the winter, and she hated the feeling of coming across the freaking freezing atmosphere of the endless nights of January and February.

Jenna liked the heat and the puny, warm wind. Summer was always her favorite season and she looked forward to it.

Soon, she stood outside the big building searching for her keys. She was heading toward the stairs when someone stopped her.

"Hi, Jenna, how are you?" he asked politely.

"Hi, John, I'm fine. How are you?" Jenna felt weird. She had forgotten that her neighbor was so handsome. She hadn't seen him for a couple of days but, the moment she smelled his aftershave, she was ready to fall into his hug. She loved his scent and she was impressed by his manners.

"I am fine thank you. I see you like jogging." John tried to be cool. He glanced at her sporty attire and smiled.

The grey pants and her white sneakers showed off her beautiful body. Then again, the pony tail that held her hair back, revealing her sweet face was another clue.

It seemed he had forgotten how to flirt with a woman too.

"Yes, I think we should all do that."

Jenna was trying to be friendly, she wanted to keep up their conversation, but she was shy. Although he seemed to be a nice guy, she wasn't sure they should get closer. Maybe they should be good neighbors and nothing more. It was too difficult for her to trust a stranger and, moreover, it was extremely difficult to trust another man again.

"I like jogging, but I like donuts as well," John said with a little laugh. He had just found the way to help her overcome the anxiety of the very first impression.

"I love donuts!" She was so excited she sounded like a little girl.

"Let's have some fun, what do you say?" John asked.

"What do you mean?" Jenna was taken aback.

"You said you love donuts." John pointed at the small café.

"I do." Jenna smiled.

He seemed really, really nice and she thought she should buy him a coffee and a donut. After all, he had helped her settle into her new home and she should return the favor. It was the least she could do to thank him for being helpful and kind.

"Then let's go," John said. He took her arm and they walked toward the shop.

***

Jenna sat in the chair, her hands shaking on the small table. She waited for the mysterious man, gazing at him. While making his order, Jenna couldn't hide her enthusiasm. Out of the blue, sweet feelings and beautiful silent questions she thought she had lost enveloped her mind.

The middle-aged man was very handsome. He was tall, muscular, cultured, and in addition, he seemed to be smart and elegant. Jenna thought that the white pants and his black jacket made him look like a hero. She really liked his style.

Then again, his silver hair and his beautiful smile pointed his maturity while his blue eyes made her think of the splendor and the serenity of the sea. John was a real gentleman and Jenna fell for his manners and the way he could affect her mood. A few weeks ago, Jenna felt as if she was standing between the Devil and the deep blue sea. Now, he could be the port to rest her mind forever.

"This is for you," John said.

"I should buy you the donut. I am here because you saved me." Jenna was impressed.

"That was nothing." He couldn't keep his eyes off her. She was the most interesting woman he had ever seen. John was impressed by her passion and thirst to do everything fast and without help. When he saw her alone outside their apartment building, trying to do everything, he admired her strength.

"If you hadn't showed up, I would definitely be in the hospital!"

Jenna was funny and her neighbor liked talking with her. The moment she took a deep breath and raised her eyebrows, while biting her lips, he was ready to laugh.

"Do you like your new home?"

"Yes, the view is incredible and my bedroom is big enough to put all my shoes and clothes!"

"I haven't seen you around, are you new to this area?" John was curious. He liked Jenna, and he wanted to know everything about her.

"Yes, and I really like this place." As hours passed by, they both wanted to find out more.

"Me too..." John loved looking into her brown eyes.

"So, what do you do?" Jenna remembered her friend and decided to follow Carla's suggestions.

"I am a teacher. I work at B.A. School."

"That's great." Jenna was surprised. She believed John was an artist, maybe an actor, or a singer.

"I would say intriguing. What do you do?"

"I am a nurse. I work at S.G. Hospital." Jenna drank some water while still paying attention to him.

"Now that's interesting." John was impressed.

"I would say tiring." For a moment, she rolled her eyes and smelled his aftershave.

Jenna felt like the first times she dated as a single woman. She used to spend five minutes to check out the candidate boyfriend. Now, twenty minutes had already passed and she kept talking with her date. She was still there, hooked by his interesting personality.

"I see. Do you live alone or...?" Was he too obvious, was he going too fast, but he was so attracted to this sweet woman. He wanted to know everything about her, ignoring the red lines during the first date.

"It's just me. I am trying to pull myself back together." Jenna sounded serious. Although she believed he should be more discrete, she answered and was honest with him.

"Let me guess, bad partner?"

"I would say the worst husband, but it's over now. He belongs to the past." Jenna sounded strong. She had overcome her ex-husband's betrayal.

"I understand." John shook his head.

"What about you, bad wife?" Jenna asked vaguely.

"I was a boring husband. But I can assure you that I have changed," John said with a little laugh.

"Excuse me?" Jenna laughed. She had never heard something like that before.

"That's what my ex-wife said." He smiled, shrugged his shoulders trying to make light of it.

"I see." Jenna drank some water while watching the interesting man.

She couldn't understand women. *This man could never be boring. He is looking for a wife to have a family* she thought.

John was seeking for a serious lady to share his life. He loved children and he wanted to have fun with the family he would make.

John and Jenna talked for hours. They discussed books, music, movies, and as time passed, they both discovered that they enjoyed the same authors, singers, and actors.

"What's your favorite song?" Jenna asked.

"Let me think. I liked Michael Jackson, so I guess *You Are Not Alone.*" John's eyes locked on hers.

"That's my favorite song too." Jenna was surprised. She didn't know what to do and she wasn't sure about what else to say.

"I call that song love at heart." John couldn't take his eyes off her. He thought Jenna was the kindest and the sweetest person he had ever come across and he wanted to spend the rest of the night gazing at her eyes. And he really wanted to do that.

"I agree with you." Jenna was confused since she liked this man, but she also believed that it was too soon to start dating. Although John was a handsome, smart man, meaning the perfect match, Jenna was not ready to move on and trust someone yet.

"I bet you like *Total Eclipse of the Heart*," John whispered.

"It's one of the best songs I have ever heard." Jenna bit her lips and rolled her eyes.

"That's pretty amazing. I finally met a young woman who likes the songs of the past." John was attracted to his new neighbor and couldn't hide his enthusiasm.

"I am thirty-five and I admire the beauty of the words, I don't like songs with catchy music and lyrics with no meaning." Jenna sounded serious.

"I'm forty-five years old and I'm glad I met you." He shook her hand while Jenna laughed.

"I think I should go home. It's too late for me." She got up and so did John.

"Thanks for being here with me," he said, smiling and waiting for her answer. He had turned red and looked like a teenager.

"It was my pleasure, John." Her facial expression made him hope for another date.

They left the small café and they both seemed happy. Jenna felt safe and liked having someone next to her side.

On the other hand, John really liked this woman.

Chapter Three

When Jenna reached her apartment and closed the door behind her, she took a deep breath and sank in her white, velvet sofa. Then, she rolled her eyes and laughed. She always loved the feeling of being lost in her house, thinking of the strangest facts of the day that had taken place in her life. Her meeting with John and their date was the best gift life had given her so far. He was so kind and he seemed to enjoy their conversation.

The night was lovely and, although spring had replaced the winter, it was a cold night. But her heart and her mind flirted intensely with the upcoming summer and its hot temperatures.

Jenna had managed to take the key of happiness back. Her neighbor had something special, and now, she looked forward to discovering all his secrets and desires. The first impression remained perfect and by the second time they met, the insecurities were fading away.

***

Her dry lips tasted the fruit salad and its delicious flavors as she looked at the yellow wall with the photos of her idols. Jenna loved the poets, the artists, and all those who used to suffer from limitless romantic inspiration. She loved reading poems while listening to the music and she never gave up on true love and romance.

The representatives of pure love couldn't keep her real company and Jenna felt lonely. And she needed someone to be next to her side as well. She wanted to reveal and share her deepest emotions with somebody that could feel the same way she felt about love.

After a few minutes, she got up from the comfortable seat and went straight to her closet. She took off her clothes as she couldn't wait to rest her body on her bed.

***

Jenna rolled her eyes and tried to sleep but she couldn't stop murmuring the same words again and again. The nasty memories of the past haunted her mind. It was like yelling at someone, *"I trusted you and you betrayed me!"*

She awoke, apprehensive, tears streaming down her face, her gaze darting around the dark room, wondering where she was.

It took long moments for her to realize she was safe and alone in her apartment. Glancing at the clock, it was just 2:30 a.m.

A tornado of emotions swept through her, forcing her from bed. She would do everything to get past the negative energy and the nasty thoughts. She loved jogging but it was too late to leave her house to start running.

What had she done by encouraging John? She couldn't trust him, could she? Jenna knew she was letting her ex-husband destroy her desires, but she was afraid she would never heal from the pain of George's betrayal. How could she trust another man when her own husband betrayed her?

She thought it would be impossible to start dating again. And she hated that feeling since she thought she was over this. If only she knew that she would have to test herself first.

Suddenly her bell rang in the middle of the night. Taken aback, she hurriedly put on a white shirt and pulled her messy hair into a pony tail while moving toward the door.

"Who is it?" She asked through the closed door.

"It's me, Jenna, John. I'm sorry if I woke you up but I heard someone yelling and I wanted to make sure everything is okay?" He couldn't stay away from her. She was a special lady and he was attracted to her. Somehow, John felt that she needed help and he should take care of her.

Jenna yanked opened the door and grabbed the man in front of her sooner than he expected. In no time, she took off his clothes and led him toward her bed. She didn't waste her time; Jenna was desperate to test the water.

Then again, there were no words to describe John's facial expression. She hoped he wouldn't mind that she took advantage of him and gained control.

John liked Jenna and he already thought he was halfway in love with the beautiful nurse.

On the other hand, Jenna was acting weird. She had turned into a femme fatale and she wouldn't let any misunderstanding come up so she was clear from the very beginning.

"It's only sex, John, nothing more"

"No. It's not only sex Jenna."

"I want only sex. Otherwise, it's the last time you come here. I need your body and nothing more. Do you understand?" She bit her lip, nervously, but was serious. That moment she really meant her words.

John rolled his eyes thinking of her words. Although he didn't know Jenna very well, he could bet she was different. He was sure she was not that kind of girl.

A couple of hours earlier, John had the privilege to escort a woman who dreamed of a world of fairy tales, waiting for the charming prince to come into her life and that was the real Jenna.

But, now, John was looking at a beautiful woman who was ready to dive under the sheets without a second thought. Her impatience to get rid of the worst part of her life had driven her crazy.

Jenna's fingers started caressing his belly as she kept stealing his kisses.

"So what do you say?" she asked.

"Is this what you really want?" John whispered as he looked into her eyes.

"Yes. This is what I really want." Jenna was ready to dare.

"Okay." He caressed her hair and kissed her forehead as she looked surprised by his gesture.

"Thank you," Jenna whispered while, immediately, feeling ashamed. By the way he glanced at her; Jenna realized that this man was not interested in having fun just for one night. He seemed disappointed.

Meanwhile, John was able to guess her thoughts. Jenna was passionate with romance and she never liked one night stands. She was against having sex with a stranger. But, now, it was too late. Moreover, her body burned with desire since she had ignored her physical needs for too long. Jenna had to let her body and mind free. She couldn't control herself.

As John stared into her eyes, he didn't lose much time and took her in his arms, heading toward Jenna's bedroom. Pretty soon, they dived into the sheets the need to satisfy their hunger for one another overwhelming. Passion ran over his flesh and now that Jenna was above him, John had difficulty breathing.

The woman was incredible. She was sexy and she knew what to do. She knew the way to make a man feel amazing.

John wouldn't miss the chance to take control and pulled her down. Jenna pulled the pillows away while John started caressing her breasts. Soon, he licked her belly and the rest of her body, spreading his kisses on her hot skin, whereas Jenna loved his moves.

Before long, he was inside her and she felt wonderful, she had missed that feeling. Her breath and her perfume made him more passionate as her sighs made him more persistent. He didn't want to stop as her kisses continued turning him on.

Jenna loved having this man inside of her. But when she closed her eyes, she remembered the past. Jenna remembered the last time she had sex. It was almost two years ago.

"I hate you, George." John stopped and looked at her. Jenna was crying.

"Who is George?"

"That's not your business, John." Jenna pulled away and stood up, leaving him alone in bed, destroying the erotic atmosphere.

"Hey, baby, it's me. What's going on?" John went hesitantly toward her side and caressed her back.

"I'm sorry, John. I can't do this." Jenna hid in his arms.

"Everything will be fine, baby." John hated pretending that he didn't mind, but decided to keep silent. He held Jenna tight.

Jenna thought it would be easy moving on, but she was wrong. Her body had said yes, but her mind insisted on killing all of her hopes of having a happy life.

They sat down on the bed and Jenna told John everything. She didn't want to let him down, but she believed she should be honest. She hated lies and she knew how it felt being betrayed. And she was also sure that John was a nice guy and didn't deserve being deceived this way.

"Fight against your fears and try to forget the past," he said as he smiled at his sweet neighbor.

John was relieved. His instincts hadn't deceived him. Jenna was a special woman, she was different.

"I will go home and I guess I will see you again," John whispered.

"Okay."

***

Jenna got up from the bed and went to the bathroom. She started crying. She had screwed up everything. She was letting George destroy her life and she felt awful. She wanted to get past his poisonous influence. Otherwise, she couldn't move on. His nasty behavior haunted her.

On the other hand, the worst part was over. She wanted to believe that his name would be deleted from every single cell of her mind because she had finally found an amazing man. She hoped and she needed to believe that she had found her alter ego.

***

John lay in his bed unable to stop thinking of Jenna. He couldn't believe there were so many stupid men out there. When he heard Jenna telling him that loyalty meant nothing to her ex-husband, he was taken aback.

He would never give up on her. He wouldn't mind if she wanted more time to come closer. He believed that sex was important to have a "healthy" relationship, covered by the blanket of harmony, but he could wait. As long as she wanted to be with him, he could be patient.

John believed that every woman needed time to heal the wounds of a separation or a bad relationship. Most women missed the phase of a relationship of knowing one another and lacked the chance to talk about love.

John was ten years older than Jenna. He was interested in finding the appropriate way to come closer to Jenna. He missed a real partner. He wanted to share the rest of his life with a caring woman who would be eager to compromise and respect the needs of her man. And he was sure he had just found her.

Chapter Four

Jenna knocked on the door of her neighbor's apartment. She felt awful and she wanted to apologize for her behavior. She had a hard day at work and she left earlier since she felt unable to deal with her responsibilities. She needed some rest and she already missed her bed, but she also wanted to make sure that everything was fine between them.

Before long, a blonde woman opened the door and Jenna froze. She tried to catch herself from showing the fear she felt. Yet, she struggled to remain calm.

"I am looking for John." Jenna hesitated. To say she was shocked was an understatement.

"He must be the handsome one." The girl was maybe twenty.

"Is he inside? Are you alone?" Jenna asked angrily.

"No, please come in. I was just leaving." The young woman smiled.

"Thank you." Jenna looked at her and tried to smile. She was hurt, disappointed, and angry enough to kill John. Jealousy gripped Jenna. The younger woman had a tight body, long blonde hair, blue eyes, and light brown skin tone, everything on her was incredible.

"I guess you will find them somewhere." The woman said.

"Okay."

She walked inside and felt weird since he should be there, guiding her into his apartment. Now, she felt she had invaded his world without his permission.

His apartment was small but, at the same time, very clean and in perfect order.

Jenna smelled the breathtaking aroma of the donuts throughout the room as it seemed like diving into the flavors of chocolate. She took a few steps, and then a glance at the empty kitchen confirmed her guessing. She assumed they were somewhere else.

She looked around her and the orange color of the walls made her feel comfortable and welcome, but as time went by; agony, morality, and discretion conquered her mind.

However, she bit her lips and looked straight at the door across the room. Undecided about invading his bedroom, but she needed to face him. He had lied to her and she was sure that the young girl was just another slut who had used him to have sex with. Jenna knew that John was a great catch and she was also aware of the female thinking. Jenna was crazy in love with him and didn't want to lose him.

Insecure, she walked to the small hall to her left. There wasn't any light in the room, but she was able to see two doors next to each other.

She decided to go into the first door in order to see him and to confirm her suspicions. She was so angry that she couldn't just ignore his behavior.

The room was totally dark while the smell of chocolate assaulted her nose. Jenna couldn't find any switch to turn on the lights but she could see the faded, yellow color below the door of a room which probably served as a spacious closet. She moved closer; her steps could barely be heard. She touched the handle, and before opening the door, she stopped. Strange sounds came through the door.

Anxious, she took a deep breath, and then leaned toward the door, putting her ear where she could hear whispering and fast breathing. The next sound seemed really familiar to her....it was the sound of having sex.

The atmosphere was full of tension and quite inappropriate, but she had to see his betrayal. Desperate to discover the truth.

Jenna felt like a bomb would burst inside her any moment.

Unable to stop herself, she opened the door as quietly as she could. Before her were two figures that were indifferent to everything around them.

Heartbroken, she slipped inside the room, closed the door behind her, and hid behind some large boxes. After a while, she slipped her head to the right side of her cover and came face-to-face with the most unexpected sight she had ever seen.

A muscular man stood naked in front of her but she could see only his back and his ass. His muscles moved under his skin. Sweat ran down his back.

The woman sat on a bench her voice trembling fast as the male carried on enjoying the intense, erotic moments by seducing her mind and body, making Jenna furious as she guessed the other woman had already managed to steal the man she liked.

Jenna guessed the other woman was completely helpless in an ocean of pleasure and guiltiness. Her feet slipped on his flank and her hands shook on the surface of an improvised bed in the burning room.

Jenna wasn't able to see his face, but she could hear him slipping into the woman she was jealous of. She could hear the sound of his lips touching hers.

Jenna was ready to show herself. She couldn't stand being treated as a naïve, little girl.

"Do you like it, baby?" He asked.

Jenna was surprised by the male's answer. She would never forget John's deep voice and she was thrilled he was not that man in front of her. She rolled her eyes and she heard the woman giving her reply.

"It's amazing," she screamed.

Jenna held her chest and tried to breathe as normally and silently as she could because she was only a step away from them. She could feel her face heat up in embarrassment as sweat covered her forehead. She felt terrible; nothing could help her deal with the shame she felt right now.

"Don't leave me yet…stay with me."

"I'm all yours," he whispered.

"I'm glad," she said.

Jenna was still there, able to smell the perfume of the man. The man who had the main role of the sex scene she was lucky enough to witness without being caught. Even if she knew it was a bit risky, she decided to have a last and quick look at them to make sure she was not mistaken. And she didn't want to lose any time.

Full of will and determination, Jenna exposed herself to see the man in his mistress's hug. They were still naked, and now the picture of them looked funny.

Jenna was relieved. She found the strength and courage to get out of the room. Despite the fact that she could have been in serious trouble if someone had seen them all together like that.

Jenna swept the sweat from her face and turned back to the living room. A few minutes later, she heard the front door open.

"Jenna?"

"Hi John."

Jenna smiled and pressed her lips together to hide the agony and the anxiety of this awkward moment. Although he was not the one who was having sex with the blonde woman and hadn't betrayed her, she would have to explain how she got in his house and the reason she was waiting for him in his living room.

"John, you are here." The blonde woman was surprised as well.

"Yes, Sara, I'm here." John looked at her curiously.

"Who is your friend?" Sara asked.

John wondered what was going on in his house.

"She is my neighbor. Jenna, this is my sister, Sara."

"Nice to meet you Jenna." Sara tried to make Jenna understand that she needed her help. She was twenty and she had brought her boyfriend in her brother's house without his permission.

John headed to the small table in the kitchen and took the mail in his hands. That moment Sara pointed at the door to make Jenna understand that they should leave for a while.

"Nice to meet you too, Sara." Jenna nodded at John's sister while the younger woman went closer.

"Could you please leave for a while? My boyfriend is here and John doesn't like him," Sara whispered.

Jenna shook her head yes and then they shook hands, trying to be cool.

"So, how are you, Jenna?" John asked.

"Would you mind going to my apartment to talk?" Jenna suggested.

"Okay." John said as his sister smiled at him and whispered thanks to Jenna for the favor.

Chapter Five

Jenna was in the kitchen of her small apartment making coffee. John was standing in front of the small window gazing at her beautiful smile.

"Which one do you like?" Jenna showed him two cups of coffee which made him laugh. He could see Mickey Mouse along with Minnie and three words, I love you. The second cup had the same picture but there were different words, I adore you.

"Let me think." He answered.

"I can wait." She said as she heard the sound of his cell phone.

"I love you." John gazed at Jenna and moments later walked to the living room to answer the call.

She had rushed to conclusions, but she realized John would never act like her ex. He was the exception to the rule. He was a gentleman.

She couldn't believe how jealous she'd been. It was the first time she had felt so attracted to a man. When she thought that John was having sex with another woman, something inside froze. At the time, Jenna was sure she could kill him.

A few moments later, John interrupted her thoughts crowding her into the cabinets. He stood in front of her and caressed her cheeks. John smiled and Jenna assumed he wanted answers.

Jenna swept her black hair off her face and squeezed her lips together to seal the secret of the guilty conspiracy.

"So, how are you?"

"I am fine. How are you?" Jenna sounded weird even to herself.

"I know the reason we are here."

"What do you mean?" Jenna was a terrible actress.

"You wanted to help my sister take her boyfriend out of my house." John took the cup of coffee in his hands and looked at Jenna.

"Listen, John…." Jenna turned red.

"It's not your fault, I know my sister." He smiled at Jenna.

"I just wanted to help her."

"That's okay," he whispered, standing in front of Jenna.

Although John looked tired, he loved being in her apartment, gazing at her big eyes and hearing her sweet voice.

They took a few steps toward the small living room and sat down in the sofa.

Her facial expression was so tempting that he wished he would have another chance with the beautiful nurse.

"I…." Jenna could smell his aftershave.

"I'm listening." John could feel her embarrassment.

"I'm sorry for my behavior. I like you, John. I really do and I want to make this work." She was so shocked because of her straightforward answer to tell him everything she felt about him. But she was in love.

"I like you, Jenna. I think I am crazy in love with you. I can't stop thinking of you."

Jenna hid in his hug while John caressed her hair.

He was ready to ask her when they both heard someone knocking on the door.

"Could you open the door?" Jenna asked.

"Of course…."

"Hi John, I came to see if everything is okay." Sara sounded curious.

"Everything is fine," Jenna said.

The two women looked at one another without saying anything more.

When John's cell phone rang, they both dove into their deepest thoughts. Jenna stared at her ideal hero.

Sara was sure Jenna was the woman who had stolen her brother's heart and mind.

"I think I'll go home and leave you two alone. I guess you need your privacy and I'm sure I'll see you later, tomorrow morning, who knows?" Sara said, teasingly. She liked Jenna and she wanted to be cool with her brother's girlfriend.

"I think you should go home." John said smiling at his sister.

"Bye Jenna!" John closed the door and turned back.

"Bye Sara." John pulled her into his arms. He felt wonderful.

The following hours they talked about everything and Jenna seemed to enjoy every single moment with him. But she was not sure about the way she should move on. She wished she could turn back the time and change the strange experience of their last meeting.

They were sitting in her favorite sofa drinking their coffee sharing promising looks.

"I'm glad you are here," Jenna said.

"I'm happy to be here," John whispered.

He seemed so kind and patient.

John could wait for her. He was interested in having a serious relationship. He wanted to share everything with a woman who would dare to love him truly and forever.

Jenna held his hand and smiled at him. The handsome teacher would be able to earn her trust. And he was the whole package she was searching for.

Jenna didn't waste time. She glimpsed down at his long fingers and then she kissed his lips. He had locked her hands in his but, after a while, he placed his hands on her legs and she liked his move.

John was speechless. His gaze was hooked on her gorgeous breasts. Her perfume had his eyes rolling in the back of his head. He dreamt of the moment they would make love.

Jenna stretched her body on the sofa. She tried to make it obvious that she wanted him. She couldn't help but smile when he got the meaning immediately.

His shoulders started loosening up and his body language changed. John welcomed the calmness and Jenna helped him find the Zen phase a few seconds later by caressing his body softly.

She looked at him while she started playing with her hair. Her eyes widened as she watched his desire grow.

"Do you want me to leave?"

"Do you want to leave?"

"I'm not sure if you want me to stay."

"I want you to stay," Jenna said seriously.

She stared at his blue pants without the slightest compunction. He seemed so strong and she couldn't get out of her mind the picture of him lying on her body. The last time they met, those hands were holding her breasts. Now, Jenna was ready to scream with passion as the level of heat flooded her body and her skin. She would do everything to have this man in her life.

She was crazy in love with the handsome teacher.

John was aware of his value and his attractiveness, he knew how to impose himself on a woman, but mostly he knew how to make everything concerning his personal life clear enough without leaving any gaps for trouble and misunderstanding. He had never exploited any woman and he had never been anything but honest. He hated playing with other people's feelings.

"Are you sure you wanna do this?"

"I'm definitely sure." Jenna pulled back her long hair and smiled.

John placed his hands on her cheeks and caressed softly her skin.

"I'm in love with you."

"So am I." She laughed, "I mean I'm in love with you."

John kissed her and Jenna started taking off his shirt. She spread kisses on his body. His aftershave was driving her wild. And his passion ratcheted her own to heights unknown.

The moment Jenna touched his chest; she felt his heartbeat beating faster than a stenographer could type. She kept caressing his body as she looked forward to making love to him.

John took off her black sweater and then he placed his arms around her waist. He began kissing her hot skin. She felt incredible. A few minutes later, he took off her black skirt, her body heated beneath his touch. He knew exactly what to do. He didn't want to rush this. He had not need to conquer her body. She was already his.

John stood and Jenna took off his pants and underwear. They fell to the sofa sharing the passion of true love and the kisses of pure romance. John started spreading his kisses all over her body as Jenna loved exploring his tight skin. They adored having their hands skimming one another's body while increasing their desire to become one, tasting the sweet flavor of a special union. They were both impatient to learn everything about their chemistry.

The handsome teacher lay on her and Jenna locked her gaze on him. The past was over. It couldn't haunt her thoughts anymore. She could see the rest of her life in his blue eyes.

Jenna placed her hands on his back and let her body and mind go free. She loved kissing him on the neck. His breath around her nape made her want to scream. The sweat on their bodies and the sounds of their union flirted with her wildest imagination. She had missed having amazing sex. She wanted to spend the whole night with her lover.

Chapter Six

"I want you to tell me everything!" Carla insisted.

"I already told you my news." Jenna knew what she would ask.

"Did you tell him?"

"What?" Jenna turned red.

"Did you?"

"I will talk to him. I just need some time." Although Jenna knew John for more than four months, she hesitated to reveal her secret.

"Okay." Carla smiled and hugged her best friend.

Usually, after work, the two friends used to have a drink and then they enjoyed going out for shopping.

The two women left their favorite bar and walked to the shops. They loved Fridays since they were both little girls and they also loved the heat and the carefree mood of everyone during the first days of August. They felt like having vacations in the most peaceful place in the world.

"I am so happy for you." Carla said.

"I know. That's the reason you are my best friend."

"Hey, girl, what is it?"

"I'm fine; it's just that I am happy and I don't want to destroy everything." Jenna was worried and confused.

"You deserve to be happy!"

"I worry about John's reaction." Tears welled in Jenna's eyes.

"John is a good man and he loves you. He would do everything for you."

"I will talk to him."

"That's the best you can do." Carla patted her back and hugged her tight.

"I will do it tonight." Jenna was determined to reveal her secret.

"That's wonderful." Carla swept Jenna's tears off her face and held her hand. She just wanted Jenna to be happy.

***

Jenna stared at the mirror in her bathroom, applying lotion to her showered body. Her breasts were covered by her wet hair while the drops of the water ran down her velvet skin. She realized her body was changing. And she had to talk to her lover immediately.

Jenna took a deep breath and tried to think of her options. She rolled her eyes, and, after a while, she looked back. In no time, her gaze was hooked by John's naked body, and she was surely aware of his needs.

John stood in front of her, smiling.

"Will you join me?" John offered his hand and, although she just had a shower, she followed him.

John breathed on her neck while, a few seconds later, the hot water started running down their naked bodies. His arms slipped on her breasts while his hands moved her black hair. His fingers softly touched her skin. She was sure he could hear the screams of need coming from her body.

Jenna hugged him tight and her teardrops managed to surprise him. She was acting weird and he couldn't explain her behavior. The last two weeks Jenna seemed different.

"Hey, baby, what's going on?"

"I am pregnant."

John moved her head up so he could see her face and, soon, his eyes locked on hers. It was the best moment of his life. He was forty-five years old and he had finally found the mother of his child, the love of his life. The sweet nurse was everything he was looking for.

"I think this is great."

"Do you really mean it?" Jenna asked searching his eyes.

"It's the best present life has given me so far. You are the best gift I have ever come across."

***

The hot water continued to fall on their bodies while they stood looking at one another. They were crazy in love and they had both discovered the road to love.

During the past they had both experienced betrayals and difficult situations, but now, they realized they were strong. They had overcome all the obstacles to reach the final destination (happiness), and both came out winners.

They would always remember the day Jenna moved to her new apartment. They would never forget their first date at the small café.

"*Miracles do happen and bear in mind that you will get what you deserve,*" they both thought and they carried on making dreams.

They had found the road to love.

What She Needs

Silent Confessions

She always hated traveling alone, she never liked being in an airplane watching the clouds in silence. All she needed was limitless love, she looked forward to finding a new partner, someone who would stand by her and would never let her fall.

The lonely woman swept the tears away and rolled her big blue eyes trying to catch her breath. The moment she pulled her long hair away from her pale face, she saw her reflection on the cold glass of the airplane window and she realized that she had to pull herself back together. She should focus on what she really needed and missed.

She would never trust another man again. She would live her life to the fullest and she would never ask for something more than physical pleasure since she regarded that no one would be able to cover her emotional needs. It would take her a lot of time to leave the nasty experience behind and move on, but she would make it, she would try to forget him forever.

Need Your Love

She loved having the young man in her life and she would do anything to make this better. Pamela had never lived something as crazy and wild as this before, and she would sacrifice everything to keep the feelings she had lost alive.

She was thrilled, she felt strong, and she looked younger than her age, always ready to share her positive energy with her friends and the people she appreciated. Pamela was an attractive woman who seemed to be happy while just having fun with men, playing their games and most times doing whatever they wanted because she always cared for her partner's satisfaction.

The last two weeks she used to smile at everyone, spreading her excellent mood through the entire city and teasing her friends. It was not a secret anymore, her body language, her kind behavior and the sweet sign of love on her face couldn't hide the truth. She never stopped smiling and waving her hands—like a little girl—at everyone who responded to the game of flirt.

Pamela was crazy in love with a younger man, but had never confessed her secret to anyone since she was shy and wanted to avoid the curiosity of her best friends who would love to know everything about her personal life. It was the first time she would dare to play with fire.

Pamela had countless talents and abilities, she could move like a jaguar—stealing the attention and the limitless admiration of everyone- but she could also be sensitive and impulsive. Although she was able to disarm her enemies and all the men who had betrayed her trust by ignoring their existence and their needs while driving them crazy and staring at them like being nothing other but zeros, she would never get past the true lovers who had made mistakes and later would apologize, begging for mercy. She never hated true lovers, she had the ability to forgive them, but she never had the least of intention of getting into new disappointments.

Pamela was able to lock her eyes on a speaker and understand whether he was honest or not, and if she really liked someone, she would always follow her heart and her instincts. Pamela was the personification of a femme fatale, a sensitive woman, but still a femme fatale.

***

The presence of the handsome man at her house had changed her life entirely. In a flash, he had managed to trigger her curiosity about his role, his interests, and had made her reconsider her living, her aspect about family life and about having a serious relationship which would last till the last day of her life.

She would never forget his facial expression during their first meeting when he stretched out his strong arm and offered his hand. He insisted on gazing at her big eyes while knowing he shouldn't have acted the way he did. That time, Pamela avoided his gaze and looked toward the white roses, but after a while, she fixed her eyes on him trying to be kind, ignoring his behavior and sexy appearance. He was a stranger, he was a kid who didn't know what to do, she was sure he had no serious plans concerning his life. But she didn't find the strength to step back and ignore him; she waited patiently under the sun's rays fighting against the heat and the sweat. At first, it was physical.

The half-naked man was different; he was impulsive—like all men in their early twenties—while he had the ability to attract her sight like a powerful magnet, making her forget her plans and dreams. The gardener had turned red; the sweat kept running down his chest as she couldn't take her eyes off his muscles. He looked like an athlete and could easily attract women. His bright blue jeans showed off his body whereas his innocent look along with his beautiful smile had already stolen her attention, turning her fears of getting older and losing her beauty into ash. Pamela felt she was the most desirable woman in the world and she really, really liked his stance. His silent flirt flattered her, and she loved having his sight on her.

Pamela rolled her blue eyes and smiled, considering the quotes about love at first sight. Out of nowhere, she had found the hope she was looking for in order to get away from the nasty cage of loneliness and, immediately, she realized that he had the qualifications to apply for the most difficult job for a man, for taking care of her heart, a woman's heart.

As an experienced woman, she could tell when she could trust someone and she was sure that he surely deserved a chance.

During their first meeting, the gardener remained speechless, he was not a boy, not yet a mature man, but he seemed to be a good man. Pamela wanted to believe that Michael belonged to the other side of modern men. She guessed he was a man who would respect the rules of romance because that was what she needed, a romantic partner. Someone who would make her feel unique, ready to risk everything for her happiness.

Pamela had never dreamed of having her own family, she always loved being a single, independent, and above all, a successful woman. She believed the whole thing of getting married was too complicated, and she never liked women who were obsessed with the idea of finding someone to have children and then asking for a divorce in order to satisfy their vanity.

Michael came into her life in the right moment at the right place. He was the one she was waiting for, he was the ideal partner, and she felt lucky they came across each other.

Pamela would never regret for putting the young man in her life, allowing him to do everything he wanted with her body. She was a woman who had never listened to what others had to say about her life, she used to ignore the rest of the world and the nasty comments.

Pamela liked living her life to the fullest; she was responsible for her own actions and never complained about anything to anyone. She used to enjoy playing with fire, as she would do anything to satisfy her needs.

When she met someone, and knew he was single, she didn't care about his past nor was she interested to interrogate him by asking countless questions. She was indifferent about words; her instincts would define the way the meeting would evolve.

For the time being, she felt weird, a wind of change had invaded her life, she was really glad she had run into the gardener.

Taking Chances

"I love you," she whispered as he kept looking into her big eyes in silence.

The weather was oppressively hot and the sweat didn't stop running down their bodies. They were making love on the bed opposite the large pool and they looked forward to getting into the water to move on while keeping the agony and the passion on hold.

The smell of the white roses, the countless diamonds in the sky, the romantic mood, and his countless kisses on her tight, tanned body had increased her excitement. She felt like a bomb ready to explode, she wanted to scream, she had already delivered her soul to him, and she would let him do whatever he wanted. In a few days, he had found the way to seduce both her body and her mind.

"I can't stand the heat," she whispered and pulled him back, waiting to see his reaction.

"No problem." The handsome gardener came closer again while Pamela found it difficult to resist. She didn't want to let him down or even suggest something different.

Michael smiled and took her in his arms as she watched him in silence, admiring his strength, hoping she would be able to lock his gaze on her eyes and her naked body forever.

***

That moment she realized she was in big trouble because she had lost her mind and she didn't care about anything other than spending all of her time with him. She was obsessed with him and every touch, every movement, every single kiss made it harder to remain steady and closer to the truth.

In a flash, she felt helpless and lonely like being alone in the ocean of life. She needed a port to feel safe, and she started wondering whether she had found it or not. Pamela was crazy in love. He could steal her attention every time he wanted and that could be dangerous because she had become weak. Pamela had no more the ability to refuse, to say no to anything he suggested. She had lost her independence because she was hooked on his desires, on his lips…

The handsome gardener had an amazing capacity to affect her soul and her body whereas she felt unable to add a word about anything. He had managed to earn her trust, her life, and her thoughts by being serious and talking when it was necessary while Pamela adored seeing herself changing, adopting his stance and affection about anything in everything. *"Live your life the way you want,"* he used to tell her, driving her crazy, stealing her heart totally.

Her thoughts were focused on him; she had become passionate with his presence. They had an excellent chemistry and nothing could separate them, not even the years, the differences and the ex-lovers.

***

The following minutes, they both looked impatient to taste the food of love again. The air of relief had covered their faces as they kept sharing temptation along with passion by stealing one another's kisses. They didn't stop teasing each other while playing in the water like children.

Pamela smiled and pulled her wet hair away from her face as he came closer and hugged her tight, making obvious his intentions.

"What do you want?" she whispered while Michael took a deep breath and sank in the water where he started spreading his kisses all over her naked body.

"I want you," Pamela said and pulled his head out of the water.

"I want you too," he said and then she bit his lips as he rushed to satisfy his needs.

They made love in the pool and didn't let anything destroy their mood. The red wine, the strawberries, and the fabulous cream had helped them find the path to euphoria whereas they were both eager to flirt with the absolute eroticism, stepping into the zone of a dangerous love.

"Where have you been?" she shouted since she couldn't stand keeping her voice down anymore.

Pamela couldn't control the passion, she couldn't resist to the crazy way he was dealing with her body. He was the best lover she had ever had and she liked seeing him playing with her agony and impatience.

"I'm here and I'm not going anywhere," he whispered as he carried on dealing with her insecurities, killing all of her doubts, and satisfying her limitless curiosity. And he continued using his strong hands, caressing her tight skin softly.

"No, you are not going anywhere," Pamela murmured, realizing she had gotten trapped in the cage of love at first sight.

She kissed his lips again and hugged him tight as they sank in the water and started swimming toward the pool stairs.

As soon as they reached the stairs, Pamela got up and moved toward the large table where she rushed to find the bottle of the red wine. Later, she looked back, locked her eyes on him, and ran toward his side again, smiling like a teenage girl while making him wonder about her plans.

Pamela came closer and, in a flash, she stood in front of him gazing at his abs and further down his body, surprising him with her action. She poured the wine on his chest, knelt, and then she started licking his body, driving him crazy, making him ready to scream. Yes, she was crazy in love with him since she had never done something like that during a first date, but she would do anything to please him. She thought it was best for her to keep her lover's interest hooked on her by using her secret talents. She had never acted that way before.

"You are amazing," he said as she moved her head up and looked into his eyes, feeling his body shaking, hearing his trembling voice.

"So are you," she murmured and continued licking his body.

They made love all night without telling him anything about their future. She pretended everything was special and beautiful as usual, although she wanted to speak up. She knew she had decided to play with fire and continued being patient even though she would love to kick him out of her house and her life once for all.

Nevertheless, Pamela abstained from revealing the truth since she had adjusted to destiny; she was destined to flirt only with the other side of love. Life had never treated her well, her parents never cared about her happiness, whereas as far as men were concerned, none had ever done something to impress her or make her feel special.

Pamela was sure there was no exception to the rule because everyone and, unfortunately, Michael as well, would never stop betraying her trust, and either she would accept the human nature or she would remain locked in the cell of loneliness forever.

She had already decided to let him discover the truth on his own, and she didn't expose her anger because she didn't actually hate him. She was able, and she wanted to forgive some of the nasty things he had done, but she couldn't forget and delete from her mind his lies.

In a few hours, she would make a new beginning as her lover would run into the consequences of his action, and she would never feel guilt for her stance.

Pamela hated lies, she felt betrayal invading her world again, remaining speechless, and seeing betrayal doing its best to turn her happiness into ash again. She had trusted him, she had trusted her instincts, and she was sure that she would never experience betrayal again.

* * *

The following morning, Pamela closed the door of her house behind her, took a few steps toward the main gate, and looked up at the sky. Out of the blue, she stopped walking; she shook her head, rolled her blue eyes, thinking about the past and everything they had shared, struggling not to cry a tear for him, and she made it. She smiled at the driver and headed toward the car while feeling confident and absolutely certain about her decisions.

The door was closed, as her eyes and her heart were sealed and her desire to forgive him flew above the white clouds of the new day. She would never come back to California, it was time to go back home, she needed to make a new beginning far away from him.

The black limo started the course toward the airport whereas her eyes remained locked on the beautiful house, watching for a last time the large trees, which surrounded the whole place and the peaceful neighborhood.

She loved that house; she enjoyed walking on the grass, looking at the large pine trees, the white roses, and the palm trees. She liked every single moment in that house since she had found the tranquility, the serenity she always searched for.

Pamela would never come back to the beautiful area and her best friends, but she was ready to make a new beginning and nothing would stop her. She would always feel blessed for knowing and sharing her time with Michael, but she loved herself as well, and now, she needed oxygen, a new change. Although the young gardener was the partner who had helped her come closer to the meaning of true love.

"Is everything okay, Ms. Jason?" The driver asked.

"Yes, everything is good."

The chapter Michael and love in California had come to an end, and she was impatient to restart her living in New York City. She would have to change everything; she would have to think of her new plans and the details of her new life in the centre of the world.

Pamela put on her sunglasses and looked like a wild rose in paradise, she looked wild and beautiful. She was a special lady, who would never compromise.

She couldn't get him out of her mind yet. She couldn't delete the first moments, the first date, and everything else they had shared since his image kept dancing in her mind.

Promiscuous

"Yes, I must be dreaming. It's not going to happen," she chuckled.

Pamela was now sure that the young man had stolen her mind. She was not able to think of anything other than his tight body and his big green eyes. She kept walking around at her luxurious house, glancing at the beautiful paintings in her stylish living room, and later, she walked outside toward the wonderful yard.

Last week, she felt weird about coming closer to her early forties, but she didn't miss the chance to celebrate her birthday with her best friends. She was forty-two years old and she looked pretty good for her age, making younger women jealous of her, trying to look like her, imitating her style and behavior. Everyone admired her long, blonde hair, her big eyes, her fabulous curves, and her sweet voice. She was exactly the woman every girl would love to become while getting older. In addition, she was smart, successful, kind, and ready to risk everything in order to feel happy, to satisfy the secret needs of her avid soul.

***

Pamela used to sink in her comfortable white armchair and liked smiling at the handsome gardener while pretending she was too busy and interested in doing everything to expand the brand name of her business. She usually laid her envelopes and countless newspapers on the large wooden table, trying to focus on her notes, the articles, reading quickly the headlines, showing him that the latest news were her only concern, and nothing could distract her attention.

When the handsome gardener took off his white T-shirt, her blue eyes locked on his muscles and she kept gazing at the sweat that ran down his white skin, feeling guilty. After a while, she glanced toward his belly and then she hooked her eyes on the beautiful white roses that surrounded the white pavilion with the white furniture, trying to seem indifferent, trying to ignore the air of attraction his body exposed and affected her spirit and body language.

Pamela took a deep breath and focused her sight on the newspapers again, struggling to adjust to reality and doing her job. She found it too difficult to get away from his charm, and his abs didn't let her base her thoughts on her business plans.

The personification of success rolled her eyes and thought of what she had achieved all these years. She knew that she was a single, beautiful woman who looked forward to meeting a romantic man, but she had no intention of giving anyone else her heart and pure feelings again.

On the other hand, his sight made her change her mind about men. That moment, she realized that what she loved most in her life was meeting challenges, and it was her right to do whatever she wanted. And she also knew that she would have no problem to steal his sight, his mind, and his heart. She was aware of her value. *Is it a crime?* she wondered.

When Pamela was younger, she was sure she would never get married, she would never have children, and she would always seek for fun and games with men who would dare to do anything for her. And she was also sure that she would become rich and successful, because that was all she wanted. Now, she had everything, but she missed a good partner, she lacked emotional stability, someone who would be able to flood her heart and her spirit with limitless love, inspiration, and positive energy.

"I believe everything is good, Ms. Jason. Do you need anything else?" Michael asked.

The young man stood in front of the wooden table like a Greek god, staring at the beautiful lady, waiting impatiently for an answer. He had turned red and it seemed that he needed some water to drink.

Everything around them was white, the flowers, the table, the armchairs, the sofas, and the huge pergola. It was the most beautiful yard he had ever seen; everything seemed so peaceful, so time traveling. It was like watching the other side of life, like seeing paradise.

Pamela loved that color; she thought it was easier to find the light in her soul while seeing her favorite things in white and she was right since she always managed to overcome problems and worries.

"Let me think." Pamela put down the newspaper, fixed her eyes on him, and noticed his long arms. When she gazed at his strong hands he had placed on his hips, she lost her control. In a flash, she stood up, surprising the young speaker who realized she was not like the girls he was dating. His boss was a dynamic woman that would get anything she wanted.

The moment Pamela came face-to-face with the gardener and smelled his aftershave, she felt the need to run to hide her guilty desires.

"I'm all ears, Ms. Jason," he said.

"Let me see what you have done," she whispered and sounded sweet and kind as always.

They walked to the stone path while the smell of the colorful roses kept following their steps, making her think of temptation and euphoria. Pamela was happy—she was attracted by a younger man, a young person who could be her son, but that didn't matter because she was crazy in love with him.

"I think the palm trees and the thymes are healthy and beautiful again," the gardener said and pointed toward the beautiful trees and the purple flowers.

Pamela liked the sound of his deep voice and she wanted to keep up their conversation, she enjoyed strolling around the beautiful house with the young man showing her his work.

"Michael, could you do me a favor?" Pamela stopped walking and took off her sunglasses.

"Yes, Ms. Jason." Michael looked into his boss's eyes and remained steady.

"Never mind, everything is excellent. Great job, Michael, thank you so much." Something inside her deepest desires made her stop talking; she hesitated.

Pamela took a deep breath and smiled, burning his curiosity, and then she put on her sunglasses again as she started walking on the wet grass trying to avoid his sight and silent questions, feeling beautiful, erotic as she used to feel in the past when she was younger, the times she flirted with handsome men.

The moment Michael looked into her eyes, she realized he had feelings about her and that could be dangerous for both of them, it could change their lives, their future. The attractive gardener tried to breathe normally again and act like an experienced man, although his cheeks had turned red and the sweat kept running down his face.

She is so hot, he thought, but didn't expose his admiration since she abstained from coming closer to him.

Then again, Pamela was taken aback by his silent stance and looked confused because she didn't know what to do. Usually, she liked taking chances, but this time, she had no idea how to deal with the promising man, she had found his reaction sweet and unanticipated as well.

Michael was in his early twenties, he was twenty-two, and also impressed by her presence. His eyes were locked on her lips, and it was obvious that he was attracted by her, but he was not sure about the next step. He remained silent and his reaction made her freeze, stepping back from a challenge she would love to accept.

"Do you need anything else to fix, Ms. Jason?" Michael asked vaguely, hearing his own voice trembling.

Pamela looked back and smiled at him. She took off her sunglasses and came closer to him while Michael was trying to find his courage and confidence as he stopped gazing at her body. He was determined to speak up and reveal everything he felt about his boss. He was in love with Pamela; he wanted to get her, and he wished they would share the night in her bedroom.

The white swimsuit and her long hair made Pamela look like the nymph of seduction. Her gaze kept playing with his imagination, tempting his body. Pamela was amazing in making things that men liked experiencing; her perfume was incredible, every time he smelled her scent through the puny air, he rolled his eyes while dreaming of the femme fatale naked in her bedroom, inviting him to her bed, and calling out for him. Pamela's new swimsuit showed off her fabulous style and shape since it left a few things covered, giving birth to his wildest and sexiest fantasy.

He was sure that Pamela had never stopped spending time to deal with herself, he knew that she loved being beautiful and having an attractive image. Love and flirt meant everything to her and she would never give up the game of love. Time was still an enemy, but kept treating her well.

"Michael, you could call me Pam," she said and smiled at him, giving him hopes.

"Okay, Pam." The gardener smiled and swept the sweat away from his forehead as Pamela raised her hand and caressed his cheek, making obvious her intentions. And it was the first time she was shaking.

That's it, I have lost my mind, she thought.

"How old are you, Michael?" Pamela asked vaguely.

"I'm twenty-two years old, Pam," he whispered as he tried to hold his boss's hand.

"I really liked your work and thank you for shaving my flowers, but now I have to go because I have many things to do. I guess I'll see you next week."

Pamela had already turned red, she had regretted her action, and now, she headed to the main house leaving him alone. Michael kept wondering about her stance and believed it was his fault that she left, he shouldn't have told her his age; he should have said he was thirty.

In less than two weeks, his boss had managed to seduce his mind and he was in desperate need of finding a way to get closer to her. He was looking forward to meeting her in private so that he would have a chance to confess his feelings.

Having an affair with an older, experienced woman and, especially with Ms. Jason, was everything he had always dreamed of. Pamela had everything he was looking for. He didn't care about her age and whatever people would say about them. She was a lady, he admired her stance, and he liked the fact that she respected herself and everyone she was coming across in her house.

"Pam," he yelled and ran toward her side.

His boss looked back and tried to remain calm since emotions and feelings she had forgotten came up, and she wasn't prepared to deal with them right now.

Pamela pulled her long hair away from her sweet face and took a few steps toward the shade of the large pine tree to protect her skin and her eyes from the sun's rays. The olive trees opposite her side stole her attention and helped her get past the agony and the tension while hearing the confession of the young man.

"Is everything okay, Michael?" Pamela asked.

"I'm in love with you," he said while Pamela froze and watched his eyes in silence.

"Did you hear what I said?" he asked a few minutes later.

"Michael." The gardener held her hand and took her in his arms where he kissed her lips and managed to surprise her.

"We shouldn't do this," she said, trying to refrain from the demands of her physical needs.

"I want to be with you," he whispered and leaned toward her hair, smelling her perfume. Then again, Pamela couldn't resist. She loved feeling his breath on her neck.

"This is insane," Pamela whispered, struggling to pull her head back together.

"We both want this. Let it happen."

The gardener kissed her lips again. She didn't step back because she liked his move. She dared to hold him tight and caressed his hair, ignoring everything and everyone in the house. She didn't care about the presence of the housekeeper and her secretary.

"Not now," Pamela stepped back and sounded serious.

"What do you mean, when…?" Michael whispered and sounded impatient.

Pamela left his hand and didn't look back while he shook his head and waited for an answer.

"I'll call you," she said and rushed to get into the house.

Dreaming of You

Although Pamela hated traveling alone, she loved airplanes. She felt like flying in the air; she felt wonderful. Right now, she would love to have someone next to her side to talk about anything while enjoying the flight until the final destination.

The moment Pamela rolled her eyes, she thought about him again and, immediately, the pained smile appeared on her sweet face, reminding her of the past and the future they could have together. When she remembered their first night, she took a deep breath and tried to get past his image since she was determined to stay away from him forever.

After a while, he managed to haunt her thoughts again since she couldn't stop wondering about his reaction. She was curious about the way he would react knowing he would never see her again, and she tried to speculate whatever he would do the following day after her decision to leave everything behind and make a new beginning without him.

***

Michael had already realized that his boss was not the usual kind of a woman. Pam was different. He was aware of her personality.

Pamela was honest and clear, he also knew that she would never forgive him because he was not sincere. Although she was sure that sooner or later he would cheat on her, she dared to flirt with him; she risked her serenity and decided to get to know him better because she believed she could trust him. And it was not his action that made her furious but his behavior.

Pamela was disappointed, she was angry with him, and lost her intense interest because he had lied to her, although she had warned Michael that the only thing she wanted for as long as they would be together was loyalty. She demanded that he be honest with her because she couldn't live with someone and share the beauty of love without knowing that it would be mutual.

Although Pamela was open-minded and regarded that it was natural to flirt with other people while being in a serious relationship in order to justify your vanity, she would never excuse the next step, she would never forgive Michael for having sex with another woman. He was younger, he was twenty-two years old, and it was a natural desire to flirt with other women too, but he could control his physical needs and behave like a real man as well. He should have respected his partner and, moreover, Michael should have appreciated Pamela for giving her love and everything she had done for him to see him happy and optimist while working hard to make his future and his life getting better.

***

"I screwed up everything," Michael whispered as he got up from the large white bed and headed toward the wooden desk opposite the large door of Pam's master bedroom.

The young gardener grabbed the envelope and started reading her letter, standing naked in front of the large mirror. In a flash, he realized that everything they had lived was over; he was free to do whatever he wanted with his life since she had no mood and intention to meet him again.

"I don't believe this," Michael murmured and sat down in the white armchair, ignoring the housekeeper and the fact that she was able to see his naked body. Michael could still smell Pam's perfume on his skin.

"Where did she go?" he asked the aged housekeeper.

"She went back home, Michael."

"Where's her home, Janet?" Michael asked again, being indifferent about his appearance; he didn't even look at the housekeeper.

"New York City," the aged woman said and left him alone while she didn't miss to close the door behind her.

"I'm not going anywhere, Pam. I love you so much, I was stupid," he whispered and avoided looking his reflection in the mirror.

Michael put on his clothes and left the house where he had experienced the best relationship of his life, while making plans for his next meeting with Pamela. He would never give up on her because she was the only one for him, the one he wanted to share his life forever.

He got into his car and stared at the beautiful house, thinking about his behavior and the way he had treated his partner.

"I'm so sorry, baby," he whispered.

Tears started running down his pale face as he realized that he had managed to ruin everything. He had shattered her heart and his lies had murdered her soul, realizing that she didn't deserve this stupid behavior. Pamela was a special woman. She never demanded anything but honesty and straight answers. She was a serious woman and she could discuss anything with anyone. If she had the chance to hear whatever he had to say about his impulsive action, she would try to understand the reasons he had had sex with another woman but still betraying her trust and limitless love.

"I wish I could turn back the time," Michael whispered again and drove away the beautiful house, the shelter he used to regard as "home," and had shared countless romantic moments with Pam during the last two months.

That house had offered him the most beautiful and unique experiences of his entire life. It was the place where he had ran into true love, respect, and appreciation. And Pamela had helped him find himself while supporting his decisions about his job and all of his future plans. She had no problem to stand by his side and see him becoming the man he always dreamed of, the man who would inspire other men do whatever he would do. Pamela was eager to give him everything he needed, and she did it. She was proud of him, but he had never seen the truth through her big blue eyes, through the mirrors of her soul.

Michael loved doing his job alone and dealing with nature, and now it was all over. He had had to think seriously his future and his life with or without Pamela.

When he met Pam, he had told her that he wanted to become a professional gardener, a new businessman who would do his best to invade the world of ecology. He always wanted to share his passion, his knowledge, and some of his secrets about the environment with other people, and Pamela had told him that she would help him achieve his goal.

In a few weeks, Michael had managed to set up his own business and, additionally, he had come across many new people who loved his work and seemed to be interested in their new friend's plans. But, above all, they loved their best friend and most of them would never disappoint Pamela.

The successful businesswoman never liked asking people and friends to do her favors, and everyone admired her stance, but Michael was the exception to the rule and his new, potential clients would never let down Pamela, their best friend, the special lady. They would risk their money to help someone they didn't know because of Pamela, they all knew she was worth it.

If only he had respected her efforts to fix things, aiming at improving his life, caring about his future. And she would do a lot more, if was an honest man.

***

She was going back home, but she didn't stop thinking about him and their first dinner.

Discovering Their Chemistry

"How about having dinner at my house? What do you think?" Pamela suggested and managed to surprise him.

Michael got up from his bed, trying to hide the joy and the beautiful smile on his face. He was shaking; his hands were trembling while his deep voice sounded weird. He swallowed and struggled to remain calm as he walked toward the small window, watching the large sycamores and the kids who liked running in the park opposite his home.

"Tonight...?" he asked and, immediately, he rushed to expose his impatience.

"Yes." Pamela said.

"I could be there in twenty minutes," he said.

Pamela laughed since she realized that he really looked forward to sharing some time together. He sounded like a teenager who was given the chance to do whatever he wanted for a whole weekend without his family's presence.

"Tonight, Michael," Pamela said and disconnected.

Michael ran to the bathroom and fought against time, he was anxious and shy, but he would dare to impress her, to steal her heart.

Mixed, various feelings and emotions enveloped his thoughts and his soul since it was the first time he would date an older, experienced woman. But he wanted to dare and he was in love with Pamela. At least that was what he believed for the time being.

The handsome, nervous gardener thought that he needed one more shower while, a couple of minutes later, he stood in front of the small mirror in his bedroom and dealt with his style. He was shaved but didn't like his haircut. After several minutes, he fixed his hair again and decided he looked good.

Michael wanted to be as good-looking as possible since he regarded that it was his only chance to earn her trust, her heart, and her interest. He believed older women hated spending their time with men who didn't care about the way they would look like, and he was determined to become the exception to the rule.

Ignoring a woman's inner feelings and female belief, he wished he would make it happen just by using his charm. He based his guessing on his previous relationships and experiences with the girls he had met in high school, and that could destroy his plans since Pamela was different. His boss was looking for a serious partner not a gigolo.

The moment Michael stood in front of the small, grey closet in his cramped bedroom; he froze in fear and looked ready to scream and shout. He leaned against the white wall and took a deep breath, striving to think of the best next step, the best way to appear at her house and seem like a true gentleman and not like a rapper. His closet lacked space and formal attire. He could only see his jeans, some uniforms, and countless T-shirts. And he didn't have the least of intention of wearing those pants.

It was obvious that he never liked suits, shirts, ties, and whatever older, elegant men used to wear. He had never thought that one day he might needed something formal, something different from the usual, sporty attire.

Michael shook his head and then looked up at the white ceiling, thinking of his boss and her beautiful smile. He was anxious as he had turned red and couldn't take a step.

"What am I supposed to wear?" he wondered and lay on his bed making dreams for the night.

What am I thinking, this woman will laugh at me, and she is probably laughing at me right now. Michael thought and hid under the blue sheets, looking for the pillows.

Yes, he was nervous, he was afraid of the very first moments of their meeting because he didn't want to let her down. He was given a chance to come closer, and he regarded that only his look mattered. He hadn't discovered the importance of honesty and being real yet.

***

As always, Pamela looked amazing and cool waiting for her guest, although she kept glancing at the huge, golden clock on the white wall. She wore a long, white dress while her long hair didn't stop playing with the puny air. She moved around the large living room like a princess while the sound of her white heels didn't stop breaking the silence. Her makeup-free face made her look natural, more attractive, and real.

The atmosphere was colored with the absolute shades of romance and the beauty of the whole place had stirred up her mood and intentions. Countless white candles, white and red roses on the table, incredible perfumes, and two bottles of red and white wines across the dining room were already set for the promising night.

Pamela seemed prepared for everything, her body language and her decisive look wouldn't let anything destroy her plans, she would risk taking the next step with the handsome gardener. She was crazy in love, and she liked the feeling of being happy and optimist all the time without a specific reason.

Her gaze focused on the beauty that surrounded the place they would spend the rest of the night and she didn't stop checking out the last details of the upcoming dinner. The backyard was full of pots with colorful flowers while the smell of the white roses carried on assaulting her nose. The large candles on the grass opposite the yard painted the night with the shade of passion and showed off the serenity of her soul, as the lights in the pool had turned the beautiful setting into a small paradise where there was only one invitation for two.

Everything was almost ready; Pamela was dealing with the decoration of the table, and of course with her favorite roses. When she placed the vase with the seven white roses in the middle of the wooden table, she heard the doorbell and rushed to welcome her guest. She wanted to make him feel comfortable, and she would do whatever was needed to see him feeling he was at his home.

"Hi, Pam," Michael said with a little laugh as he sounded nervous.

"Hi, Michael." She offered her hand and, immediately, she felt the sweat in his palm.

"You look different, and more handsome," Pamela said, trying to help him overcome the anxiety of the very first awkward seconds.

"You look wonderful. You are so beautiful," Michael whispered and gazed at her big eyes, trying to breathe normally. He had no words to describe her perfume; it was incredible, an incredible scent of vanilla.

"Let's go outside." Pamela pointed at the backyard and Michael moved on as she followed him back.

The gardener was impressed. He had never seen the large living room and the rest of her house before, and he didn't know that his boss had an admirable style in everything. He knew nothing about decoration, but he was sure she had done a great job. He could stand there for hours watching the luxurious furniture and the strange but beautiful paintings.

"Would you like some wine?" Pamela asked and fixed her eyes on his grey suit, trying to be discrete.

"Yes."

Michael had decided to put on one of his father's suits, but he looked awful. Either his father would have to lose some weight or Michael would have to buy new clothes. Nevertheless, Pamela didn't deal with his appearance nor did she make any comment because she knew that she would make him feel embarrassed. She could see him behaving nervously like a fish out of water, she could understand that he was anxious, and she had realized that he had tried really hard to appear at her house like a real gentleman. And she respected the fact that he really tried.

"You are so beautiful, Pam" Michael said.

"Thanks." Pamela smiled at him and offered him the drink.

"It is summer solstice. The first day of summer," he said.

"I'll drink to that!" Pamela sounded sweet and lovely.

"How was the rest of your day?" he asked and Pamela seemed surprised. She thought he would rush to have sex with her. Instead, he was interested to find out how was her day.

"You know the same as usual. Please, have a seat," she said and wondered about his attitude.

"Do you cook?" Michael asked while looking at the plates.

"Yes, I like cooking," Pamela said.

"I'm sure it's perfect. I like the smell and I love spaghetti."

"I'm so glad! Are you hungry? Would you like to eat?" She gazed into his eyes and she managed to seduce his desire since he just nodded at her.

"Yes, sure." Now Michael couldn't take his eyes off her. He liked watching her serving him.

Later, anxiety took over again since Michael found it difficult to pick up the right fork. He had never understood the reason people needed so many forks, knives, and spoons on the table. He thought one fork, one spoon, and one knife were enough to eat everything.

"You can use whichever you want, no need to worry about it," his boss said with a little laugh and he smiled.

Pamela liked seeing him doing his best to adjust to her world. She locked her eyes on him and watched his moves in silence, trying to make out whether he felt comfortably or not. She was interested for him, but she would never admit that she was in love with him. Michael had made her lose her mind, she was out of control, and extremely happy that he was there, next to her side.

Michael had an amazing ability to help her stay calm and having fun, and he didn't let her feel bored at all. His presence had triggered her desire to get to know him better as his ignorance about many things had become unbelievable and intriguing as well. She regarded she could be his mentor whereas their chemistry would give birth to a powerful combination. They were totally different, there was a huge gap concerning their ages since Pamela could be his mother, but she didn't care because the attraction kept increasing, driving both of them crazy and that was mutual. Pamela was eager to teach him everything he needed.

Michael was young, active, and full of energy, thirsty to learn and to know many other things, whereas his attractive boss had earned his respect. She was the most appropriate person to show him everything and guide him everywhere he wanted.

"I love the pool," Michael said.

"Have you ever swum in the pool? Do you have a pool?" Pamela asked vaguely.

"No and no. I live in a small house with my parents and having a pool like this one is just a dream and since nothing is for free, I guess you can understand that we can't afford it," he answered and looked toward the pool again.

Pamela shook her head and pulled her hair away from her face, feeling uncomfortable.

"Do you have a girlfriend?" she asked.

"No, I don't."

"Why is that? You are handsome, you have a job, and you seem like a nice guy. I am sure you could find a good girl," Pamela said, pretending she was cool. She was struggling to hide the anxiety behind her laugh, although her voice sounded weird, different.

"I guess I'm just strange."

"What do you mean?" Pamela hooked her gaze on his lips.

"I don't like girls, I like women." Michael smiled and caressed her fingers while Pamela blushed. He had a unique way of making her feel special. A touch, a smile, and a few simple, beautiful words were enough to skyrocket her to heaven.

"I see."

Pamela put the fork and the knife down, and got up from her seat, and later, she took a few steps walking toward the pool. Then, she turned back and gazed at him.

"Are you coming?" She pulled her hair back and took off her dress and her shoes.

Pamela remained steady while Michael, startled by her actions, looked as cold and lifeless as a statue. She was naked and looked amazing as her perfume kept spreading through the whole place, waking up his body, triggering his desire. Pamela was fabulous and she was willing to surrender, soon she would belong to him.

"The weather is oppressively hot. I can't stand the heat," she whispered and dove into the water.

Michael stood up, and in a flash, he took off his clothes and walked to the pool too, ready to meet the biggest challenge of his life.

Pamela was looking at him, and waited for him to join her. She bit her lips and smiled at him whereas he felt blessed, he seemed to enjoy this evening since he had his chance and everything was great.

"Don't you like swimming?" she whispered but that sounded like begging him to get into the water. Her sight was locked on his naked body and she was impatient to move on, risking everything.

"I like swimming and I like you too." Michael walked around the pool heading toward her side and later knelt in front of her when she kept coming closer.

"I like you, too." Pamela caressed his legs and the rest of his body, and for a while, she hid her head between his legs, licking his skin, driving him crazy.

Michael touched her hair, caressed her sweet face, and smiled at her while she pulled him in and dragged him near her side, inviting him to have fun into the water.

The following minutes, they acted like children who loved playing in the pool, and it was obvious they both enjoyed teasing one another since they were hesitant to dare. Every time Michael was trying to come closer to Pamela, she avoided him, increasing the passion and his impatience. She could see that he was attracted by her, but she was still afraid to risk too much.

Michael was handsome and had an amazing body, but she also knew that she was playing with fire. This man could destroy her life forever, although he had everything a woman was seeking. And she was already in love with him—a very dangerous proposition.

"I think everything is amazing," Michael whispered.

The city lights stole their attention; the view from the pool toward the city was incredible. The house was located on a hill, which was surrounded by countless large trees, and only from the pool, everyone could stare at the lights and enjoy the greatest view.

The stars and the city lights had turned a romantic evening into an extremely erotic night where neither of them could resist tasting new experiences.

Pamela swam away from him and rested opposite his side where she placed her hands on the white tiles showing off her fabulous body. A few meters separated her from the personification of the absolute happiness and she carried on resisting, but in vain. She would let this man do whatever he wanted with her body.

"Yes, indeed," she whispered.

Michael swam slowly toward her side, and soon, she was able to see him in front of her, ready to get her. They were face-to-face and she started shaking, but she loved his move. The moment he raised his hand and pulled her hair away from her blue eyes, she froze; she felt euphoria running in her veins.

"You are so beautiful," he murmured.

"So are you," she said.

Michael came even closer. His body touched hers.

"I demand loyalty and honesty," she whispered and rolled her eyes as he made obvious his passion, revealing his intentions on her body.

"I'm your man," he whispered and softly bit her lips.

"Don't hurt me."

Michael kissed her lips and she hugged him tight. She loved feeling his chest on her breasts and she adored feeling his passion on her belly.

"I promise I won't hurt you." The gardener spread his kisses on her body and later sank in the water where he started gently biting her nipples, driving her crazy.

Pamela wanted to scream, she wanted to let everyone know that she was crazy in love with the young man, and that she had given him the permission to do anything he wanted with the temple of her soul.

The following minutes, Pamela managed to slip and got away from him, as she kept teasing him. She swam toward the stairs of the pool, and Michael rushed to pull her under. It was his chance to earn her love and trust. He bit her lips tenderly; her neck, and then he started licking her breasts. Soon, he went further down and she felt ready to explode.

"Let me take over," she said.

Michael sat back and liked her stance since he enjoyed watching her doing her magic things in agony, playing his mistress's game. He was thrilled; Michael was excited and couldn't wait any longer.

"I have to pick it up," she said and stood up, surprising him.

Pamela got out of the water and headed toward the white table to answer the call. She had to take care of everything.

"No, you don't have to pick it up." He hated mobile phones and those who had nothing other to do than annoying people who were trying to have sex and fun while looking impatiently for some time to get away from everything to relax.

"It's a serious call." Pamela sounded serious.

"I demand your attention," he said and gazed at her big blue eyes.

Pamela put the cell phone down, smiled, and jumped into the pool again while Michael followed her back. She tried to play with him, but when he cornered her, she realized it was over. She used her legs to avoid him, but Michael dived into the water and later appeared in front of her, pressing his body on hers. Pamela froze and let him do whatever he wanted. The gardener kissed her lips and held her hands.

Pamela felt his passion; she liked watching his eyes as he invaded her world. She was not panicked, no… not anymore, although she was still afraid of the consequences of their union. Nevertheless, she loved his move and she was ready to beg him not to stop.

Michael got in and finally conquered her body, delivering her heart and her soul to the young man. Pamela squeezed her legs around his waist, as he kept getting in, deeper and deeper.

It was the best sex of their lives and they had just discovered that their chemistry was too strong. They would do anything to protect their affair.

Killing Me Softly

In less than two hours, she would be back home, back to New York City, the place she always loved and regarded as her home.

Pamela was sure that the sleepless city would help her get past his betrayal and everything else relating with the young gardener. She would never forgive the lies, the way he had treated her, the way he had murdered her feelings thus shattering her heart. She rolled her eyes and the past haunted her mind.

***

Pamela had seen Heidi, her secretary, flirting with him, but she could never believe that she would actually dare to steal her boss's boyfriend.

When Pamela saw them having sex in her own house, in her living room, she lost her mind. She was ready to rush into the room and kill both of them. Instead, she closed the door of her own house behind her and she left. After several walks in the City of Angels, she realized that it was not only his fault, and she did nothing other than trying to forgive him for sharing his body with another woman. The same night she went back home and said nothing, Pamela pretended everything was the same as usual and she didn't say no to Michael. She waited to hear him saying sorry, she slept with him, although she hated having his body on hers, and she never heard the word she wanted and needed to hear.

The following day, she fired Heidi and didn't even look at her the moment she left her office. Her secretary kept begging for another chance while wondering about her decision. She didn't have the least intention to confess her adventure with the gardener since she knew her apology wouldn't be accepted by the impressive blonde woman.

Pamela was open-minded, but she was crazy in love as well, and she hated knowing that her partner liked having sex with other women. She wanted to feel unique, she needed to know that she was the one, the only one that Michael loved sharing his body with and living his life.

In truth, the fact that the handsome gardener had lied to her had already caused a lot of pain and had started destroying their relationship. The way he had acted had made her change her mind about the man she had put in her life, and she could do nothing to get his betrayal out of her mind.

If he was honest, and if he had shared his thoughts with her, she would be able to forgive him, and she would try to make a new beginning again. But Michael had never told her anything, he had hidden the truth, murdering her soul and trust. In addition, he didn't dare confess the truth and didn't try to apologize for his behavior. He never said anything about the sin moments he had lived with Heidi, and that killed Pamela. She waited for more than two weeks for his confession, but he was acting like nothing had happened, and she wouldn't spend her life with someone she would never trust.

***

The lonely woman opened her eyes and thought of the very first moments, the beautiful moments she had shared with Michael in California.

***

"I think this is nice," Pamela said, pointing at the grey jacket.

"It's nice, but I can't afford it." Michael said and stepped back, feeling embarrassed as he turned red and held her hand, heading toward the square.

"Do you like it?" Pamela asked and made him stop.

"Yes, I like it but what's the point? I told you, I can't afford it," Michael said with a little laugh and held her hand, taking a few steps.

"Let's go in. I want you to put on that jacket, I want to see you wearing it," she said.

"What…?" he asked when they were already in the shop and everyone was watching them.

"Put this on. This jacket is perfect. You need some suits."

Michael turned back and gazed at the manager who smiled at him while Pamela insisted on seeing him wearing the blue suit and the grey jacket.

"Pam, I told you that I can't afford this," Michael whispered and acted like a child. He looked into her eyes and then squeezed her hand in his palm.

"I'll buy you the suit and the jacket, see it as a gift," she whispered.

"No."

"Michael, can you do me a favor? Please put on this jacket." Pamela sounded serious and she wouldn't step back. The moment she took off his black jacket, he realized there were no negotiations.

"I can't do this." Michael took a deep breath and smiled at Pamela.

"Do you love me? Do you like being with me?" She asked and looked into his big green eyes.

"What kind of question is that? Of course, I love you and I like being with you." Michael sounded angry, he didn't expect these questions, and he felt emotionally trapped.

"Then let me buy these clothes for you! Wouldn't you do something for me?"

"Yes, but it's not the same," he murmured.

"When you become rich, you'll buy something for me, okay?" Pamela smiled and hugged him tight, ignoring the rest people while he shook his head and kissed her lips. He realized there was no way to leave the place without buying the clothes she liked, and he knew they were perfect too. He liked the clothes.

"Okay," he said and walked to the dressing room.

Later that night, they spent many hours' together, sharing intense erotic moments. They made love in front of the fireplace on the white carpet and seemed to enjoy the sound of the rain on the yellow tile roof. The sweat ran down their bodies as they kept releasing the sounds of the absolute pleasure from their lips.

New clothes, shoes, bags, a new iPhone, and a new laptop were lying on the beautiful sofa whereas Michael's new car was outside Pamela's house. He had everything he had ever dreamed of, and of course, the best sex in his life. That woman was willing to offer him everything; she was not hesitating to prove her love, to expose her feelings.

Pamela swept the sweat away from Michael's face while he kept dancing on her body. Then, she started screaming but none could hear her since the strong wind swept her screams away. She loved having this man seducing her body, lying on her skin, licking her breasts, and kissing her neck. She had never found it so difficult before to control herself and to keep her voice down while having sex.

The handsome gardener had managed to block her insecurities and had also helped her discover the other side of her extreme and limitless passion. All she wanted was sharing her life and all of her time with him, ignoring everything and everyone else around her.

Although she thought relationships never lasted for too long—she believed they were like fireworks—she kept investing on him and she would never regret for her decision for moving on with Michael and putting him in her life, and in her bed.

Pamela had decided to offer him anything he needed and her next goal was to see him achieving his professional goal. She would do anything to see him standing on his feet. Setting up his own business would be the next step to bolster the confidence he lacked. Somehow, she regarded that no matter what, she ought to protect him and show him the path to another world—the world of the rich and famous where he would have the comfort to enjoy everything they desired.

As an experienced businesswoman, she would have no problem showing him the path to success and wealth. She had found the way to make women all over the world trust her brand and buy the products she loved promoting. Setting up a small business for her boyfriend was just a piece of cake, and soon, she would meet her next challenge.

Pamela had managed to build her brand name in clothing and she knew the way to do it again for the man of her life, for the handsome gardener who had stolen her mind.

"I love you," he whispered.

"I love you too," Pamela murmured.

"You are the best thing that has ever happened to me," Michael confessed and looked into her big blue eyes.

"Stop teasing me. Don't talk too much. It was great sex, but don't say things you don't really mean," she said and laughed at him.

"I'm just saying the truth," he said.

"Are you serious?" Pamela pulled her hair back and sounded curious; she loved what she had just heard.

"Yes, Pam, I love you, and I 'm crazy in love with you." Surprised, she bit his lips and stared into his eyes. She was so happy.

"I am crazy in love with you too." Pamela was taken aback; she leaned on his chest and locked her sight on the white ceiling. She had confessed her secret; she had told him how she really felt about him, and that made her worry. She was still fighting against insecurities.

"I want to spend the rest of my life with you," he whispered.

"I want this too," she confessed, and now, she felt peaceful. It was the first time she actually believed that miracles do happen every day.

Being Real

Michael was staring outside the window of his small bedroom at his house thinking of Pamela and the way he had treated his partner. The cold glass reminded him of the nasty moments of the nasty past when he had fun with Heidi, cheating on his partner. If only he could turn back the time. He would do anything to change everything; he would say no to Heidi, he would have done something to prevent this from happening. And he could have been honest.

Michael had never acknowledged his behavior nor had he said sorry like he should have done. Pamela was not a stupid girl, she always respected him and appreciated his presence in her life, and every time she had the chance to prove it, she always did it without hesitating to be real.

He had never asked any questions about Heidi's absence, and had never wondered about her silence for days. It meant nothing for him, it was just sex, but it was enough to destroy their future. As time passed by and Pamela was gone, he realized what had happened. He was just another liar who had betrayed her trust.

"I miss you so much, Pam," he whispered as he rolled his eyes, wondering about her new beginning.

Michael put on his grey jacket and got out of his room, heading toward his office, eager to forget his worries by doing his job.

Pamela had made his dreams come true and now he had his own business, he was dealing with nature and gardening, and he had employees and a great team sharing his passion and doing what he did. Michael had become a responsible man, a new businessman, and all that was made possible under Pamela's guidance and protection. Now he was able to decide for his business, he could do whatever he wanted, and that was because he had the privilege to keep in his hands a special woman's heart. She didn't want revenge, she could destroy him, but she was not that kind of girl…

Michael got in his car and checked out his mobile phone, hoping to see a call or a message from his ex-girlfriend, but nothing. Pamela was gone, she would never come back, and he had to accept the truth.

Nevertheless, his thoughts remained sealed in the closet of the sweet past. He had missed the times they were walking hand in hand on the streets, glancing at the shops, having fun like all the couples, talking with the pedestrians.

He would never forget the times he wanted to show off his courage. He smiled as he recalled an unpleasant fact while dating his boss.

***

"Pam, how are you?" The good-looking, middle-aged man offered his hand and smiled at Pamela.

"Hi, Robbie, I am fine thank you. How are you?" Pamela was taken aback, as soon as they shook hands, she turned red and felt uncomfortably, avoiding Michael's gaze.

"Hi, Robbie, I'm Michael, Pam's boyfriend." Michael shook hands with Robbie while Pamela watched both of them in silence, feeling weird. It was the first time she felt she belonged to someone.

"Pleased to meet you, Michael," Robbie said with a little laugh and stared at Pamela. Later he felt like a loser and remained silent.

"The pleasure is mine." Michael turned his sight toward Pamela and held her hand.

"Nice seeing you again, Robbie," Pamela whispered and squeezed Michael's hand, heading toward the main square of S. George City for shopping.

The following minutes they said nothing, they both abstained from making any comment, although Michael was curious about Robbie, but being sure that he was Pam's ex-lover. Then again, Pamela fought against her insecurities and stupid fears. She had a past like Michael and she loved living her life the way she always wanted.

However, she liked the fact that Michael made obvious their connection; she loved seeing Michael finding his confidence and being proud of having her in his life, next to his side.

Pamela felt weird since it was the first time she dated a man so young and she was afraid people would judge her for her decisions. Everyone would gossip her all the time. But, later, one glimpse toward her boyfriend was enough to help her realize that she really enjoyed Michael's presence in her life, and she cared for nothing but her own happiness.

"Who was Robbie, Pam?" Michael couldn't stand remaining cool and indifferent, he sounded annoyed.

"A good friend. He's a nice man," she said.

"Did I say something that made you feel uncomfortable?" Michael asked vaguely.

"Why are you saying that?"

"When I said to your friend that I'm your boyfriend, you turned red and avoided his sight," Michael said and stopped walking.

"To be honest, I didn't expect that answer," Pamela answered and stood in front of him.

"Are you ashamed? Am I your boyfriend or not?" Michael sounded curious and disappointed.

"You are my boyfriend," Pamela said and caressed his black hair.

"Prove it," he said.

"How? What do you mean?"

"Hug me tight and kiss me so everyone knows I'm your boyfriend."

Pamela laughed and took off her sunglasses. Her bright blue jeans and her white shirt showed off her beautiful, tight body and made her look like a teenage girl. Then again, Michael's sporty, black attire showed off his muscles, he looked like the perfect match for Pam.

"Are you serious? she said with a little laugh.

"Yes, and I'm crazy in love with you."

Pamela hugged him tight and softly bit his lips. She kissed him while the pedestrians and the drivers of the noisy city honked at them, smiling, and clapping their hands.

The sun's rays and everyone's attention were locked on them, but they were indifferent since they were meant to be together and nothing could separate them.

"Are you happy now?" she whispered.

"Yes, I am," he said and held her in his arms.

"I don't care what others will think about us," she said.

"Neither am I." Michael was honest and still held her tight.

"And I am proud of you." Pamela kissed him again, surprising her partner.

"You are my baby, Pam." Michael rolled his eyes and delivered his soul to Pamela.

The path to heaven was intoxicating; he was addicted to her smile and her beauty. He had never thought he would find his peace, the serenity he was looking for in his relationship with Pam.

She was the best present life had given him so far and he felt blessed and lucky. But he would not keep his promise.

A Safe Shelter

Pamela had really missed her home, her private shelter, and her favorite city. She needed time to pull herself back together, find herself again.

The moment she stepped into her home, she felt loneliness coming closer to her soul since the last time she had visited New York. Michael was with her, making her happy. That time, the beauty and culture of the sleepless city had amazed him.

Pamela walked to the large, white living room and stood in front of the wet glass of the large window where she glanced at the skyscrapers wondering about the past, the cold weather, and the rain that had brought them closer when they were together, and had made love while watching the incredible view toward Central Park.

She rolled her eyes and remembered that she had plans; Pamela wanted to meet her friends since she had missed having a good time, and right now, she needed to forget his existence.

When she turned back and gazed at the white sofas, she felt like a stranger in another world. She felt lonesome again and the lifeless atmosphere made things worse. His memory, everything they had done there, and his smile would haunt her thoughts for too long.

The next day, she had the same problem again, but after a week, she got past his short presence in her life and started adjusting to reality. Her daily program at work and the countless responsibilities helped her overcome the painful separation. But the nights carried on making her life difficult.

It was three in the morning when she woke up, and he was there again.

***

"Do you like it?" Pam asked.

"It's perfect. Thank you so much for this trip. I always wanted to visit New York." Michael took off his jacket and stood in front of the large window, watching the whole city from the penthouse of the modern and luxurious apartment building at the most famous and expensive avenue of New York. He had no idea Pamela was so wealthy, and he didn't really care. He was never interested about her bank accounts, at least he was man enough to trust his own hands and depend on himself.

"You don't have to thank me," she whispered and let him enjoy the view.

"Do you have to go to work?" Michael asked.

"No, not today. Why do you ask?" Pamela asked.

"I think it would be great going out, going to the theater," he suggested as Pamela shook her head and seemed surprised.

"Would you really like that?" she asked.

"Yes, baby."

"After showing you how beautiful you are," he whispered.

"I want you to show me," she said and they made love like the first time they met.

A few hours later, they looked like they had been stranded in paradise.

The night had blanketed the entire city as the snowflakes had covered their hair, playing with their carefree mood. They were smiling, they were happy, and they loved spreading their positive energy, living every single moment like being the last one. And they looked like a really happy and beautiful couple since they held one another and walked on the streets hand in hand, whispering sweet confessions to one another's ear.

"Are you happy with me?" Pamela asked.

"No need to ask me again. I'm very happy with you, Pam. I love your smile, your big eyes, and the way you are always taking care of everything. I need you and I want you in my life because you showed me the path to happiness and serenity. Are you happy with me?" Michael sounded like a small boy.

"Yes, I am."

"Do you mean it?" Insecurities came up and covered his thoughts.

"Yes, Michael, I mean it. Now come in!"

They sat back in the white sofa at her apartment and drank their drinks, talking about their lives and their futures.

Pamela was ready to confess that she would stay with him for the rest of her life. She was focused on her partner and she loved listening to him. Every time he talked about their personal life he used to say "we" and not *"You"* or *"I."* That made her believe that she had become a part of his life, showing Pamela that he had feelings for her, cultivating her heart and spirit with limitless love, looking forward to meeting all the magic they would ran into in future.

Apology

"I'm sorry I lied to you," Michael said.

"What are you doing here?" Surprised, Pamela shook her head and looked back. She was ready to go into her apartment building.

"Would you be able to forgive me?" Michael looked awful. He had lost weight and seemed sleepless and tired. His messy hair and his big, swelled eyes made her feel sorry for him.

"Why did you do it?" Pamela asked and took a few steps toward his side. She stood in front of him, waiting for an honest answer.

"I thought you would break up with me. I believed you would get rid of me since I had nothing to offer you," Michael whispered and offered his umbrella to cover her head from the raindrops.

"You offered me love and happiness. Why should I break up with you?" Pamela sounded sweet and lovely as always.

"Give me another chance, baby." Michael raised his hand and touched her face as she looked into his eyes.

"Why, Michael, and please be honest with me." She sounded serious and angry, and she didn't care about the rest people around them who kept watching them.

"I miss your smile, the sound of your sweet voice, and the way you hold my hand. My life is empty and I don't think I'll manage to overcome our separation. All I need is a second chance and I promise I will fix everything. I'll be the person you came across that beautiful day I came to your house to clean your garden. I will remain the gardener you fell in love, I am your man," he murmured.

"Michael, I need some time to think," she said, struggling not to cry.

"I understand. You need time. I'm here to tell you that I can wait." Tears ran down his pale face.

"Take care."

Pamela got into the building and rushed to hide in her shelter as he kept looking at her. She was so beautiful; she was amazing.

A few minutes later, Pamela was living the worst nightmare. Her mind was saying no, but her heart was saying yes.

She leaned against the large window and looked up at the clouded sky and the crazy raindrops as the tears started running down her sweet face, covering her pained smile. She cared a lot about Michael, but she was no longer eager to be with him because she would never trust him again. As much as she needed his hugs and his kisses, she couldn't forget the past. It was not easy to forgive him and make a new beginning with him.

***

Michael kept walking in the rain, thinking of his walks with Pamela in New York City. That woman had helped him find himself while discovering new things in his life.

When he reached the small café across Central Park, he sat back and stared at the beautiful lake, thinking about the moments they had spent there.

He swept the raindrops away from his face and rested his sight on the lake and the large trees that surrounded the park. The countless children that visited the place took the sadness away and showed him the path to calmness, forgetting his worry for a while.

Michael had made the worst mistake in his life. He had regretted his behavior, but he didn't apologize when he should have. Although it was not the time to place the blame since he couldn't stand the truth, he would never forget what Pamela had done for him.

Out of the blue, Michael got up from his seat and grabbed his bag. Despite the noise and the presence of the people in the small café, he heard the sound of his cell phone and rushed to get it in his hands.

"Where are you?" Pamela asked.

"At the small café across Central Park," he said.

"I'll be there in a few minutes," she whispered and disconnected.

Never Be the Same Again

Pamela called a taxi and headed to her favorite place while thinking of their very first meeting. It was many months ago, the first days of June.

***

Pamela had returned back home earlier, while Michael was dealing with the grass. The gardener had taken off his T-shirt and sweat ran down his skin, stealing her attention. His big eyes and his tired smile showed off his beauty, and she felt nice seeing him in her house.

"I think I haven't seen you before, I'm Pamela and I like your work," Pamela said and stood in front of him, introducing herself.

"Thank you," Michael whispered and held her hand.

"Pamela Jason." She sounded friendly and smiled at him.

"I'm Michael Lison," he said.

"Pleased to meet you, Michael," Pamela said as the gardener nodded at her, trying to overcome the anxiety and the shock. He had heard from the personnel of the office where he had applied for the job that Ms. Jason was a very beautiful woman, but he didn't believe them, and that time, he didn't care about it.

Pamela remained in the beautiful yard and gazed at him while he did his work. That man had something special, something that she couldn't explain, and that something had stirred up her thoughts and interest. She was determined to get to know him better, and twice a week— the days the gardener was supposed to be at her house to clean the garden—she worked from her home. Three weeks later, she was ready to dare and give him the chance to earn her trust and love.

Now she had had to think seriously whether she would give him another chance or not.

***

"Hi," she whispered as she reached him.

"Hi, Pam," Michael sounded weird. He stretched out his arm and she sat in the chair, watching his hands and his fingers. Michael was shaking; a torrent of tears formed on his face, exposing his pain and revealing his true apology.

"You didn't have to come to New York," she murmured.

"I'm sorry, Pam. I was a fool. I don't know why I did it. I love you, please forgive me." He couldn't control his feelings, he was suffocating, and he would never overcome their separation. And he meant it.

"Michael," Pamela cried out and hid her face on his chest.

"I'm so sorry, baby." He placed his chin on her head and held her tight.

"You hurt me." Pamela was confused and didn't know what to do.

"I know that and I'm terribly sorry," he murmured.

"I guess love hurts." Pamela locked her eyes on him and sounded like a little girl.

"I want to know what love means, and I want you to show me again."

Pamela moved up her head and kept watching his eyes, wondering what to do, looking for an answer. She was still crazy in love with him and she already knew the answer he was waiting for.

The snowflakes started dressing the whole place as they were still inside the small café gazing at the park and the people.

Pamela hid in his hug, and it felt nice. She had missed having his arms around her. She had missed his scent and his presence. She needed him in her life.

Michael heard what he wanted, but Pamela never trusted him again. The moment she had come across his betrayal, she stopped having the feelings she had about him. She loved him because he was a good man, a good friend that was also her lover. She didn't count on him anymore. He was free to do whatever he wanted. She had realized that Michael was not her possession.

Pamela couldn't ignore the difficulties they would come across in future. She was getting older, he would cheat on her in future, but she had already accepted that because she was able to find her peace. She had come across the other side of love where you can love someone and accept the level and the type of love you are offered.

They were happy, they shared wonderful moments, and they seemed eager to spend the rest of their lives together.

La Vie Este Belle

"Are you happy, Pam?"

"Yes. I am the happiest woman on earth," she whispered while looking into his big eyes.

"Will you stay with me forever?" he asked, holding her hand tightly.

"Yes, I belong to you and you belong to me."

"Thank you so much, Pam. You can't imagine how happy you made me. I will never forget your trust and love."

"Baby, you showed me the path to life again. I am not a fool. I want to share everything I have with you."

Pamela came closer and kissed his lips, whereas he felt like stepping into the paradise. Michael was living the most exciting experience in his whole life and would do anything to make this better. He had earned her love and appreciation again; he had run into a woman who was eager to offer him everything he needed. And Michael was not the same man, he had changed, he was another man; he was with her enjoying great sex, love and freedom.

"Let's go back home, back to California," she said.

"No, let's stay in New York, but let's focus on where we are today. This is the first and most beautiful day of summer. It's the twenty-first of June you know. It is summer solstice. It's been a year since life brought us face-to-face," he whispered and she smiled.

"I'll give you everything you want, Michael."

They stopped strolling and the young man rolled his eyes and placed his hands around her waist.

"I want to be with you. This is the best place I have ever been."

The sunlight showed off her fabulous, naked body, which had already stolen Michael's mind and heart. She was the most attractive woman he had ever come across and he would never let her go. And for the time being, he was only interested in living his dream, they had never been to Maldives. They were alone in a small, beautiful island living the best moments of their relationship.

Pamela caressed his hair and locked her eyes on his. They kissed and shared the passion they both felt, getting ready for a night that would allow them to release their wild instincts.

Michael started kissing her neck and made obvious his intentions as his naked body couldn't stand resisting. The warmth of her body had turned his mood and desire into the greatest temptation; he wanted to get her right here right now.

Pamela held his hand and took a few steps toward the sea, as he seemed unable to say anything. He followed her back and looked forward to having sex with her again.

The following minutes, they were in the water where Pamela kept spreading her kisses on his body, driving him crazy. The young man was looking up at the sky, releasing the sounds of the absolute pleasure.

Michael was living the wildest erotic moments ever and couldn't even move. He loved feeling her hands, her fingers, and her wet hair on his belly and the rest of his body. In less than two days, that woman had managed to capture his spirit by using her body language, forgetting everything.

"I want you," he said and rushed to hug her while she let him do whatever he wanted and delivered her body to his avid physical thirst.

"You are mine, Michael. Don't hurt me again," she said, as he remained speechless, making love to her, feeling incredible having her breasts on his chest and watching her big eyes.

"Never again, baby and that's a promise. I'm yours and you are mine," he said.

The setting was divine, the temperature of the water was perfect, and the beach they were stranded on was incredible. The location was breathtaking, beyond everything he could have ever imagined.

Michael believed he had found everything he missed and didn't want to ruin the most intriguing moments fate had decided to offer him again. Their relationship kept evolving; it was love at first sight along with a mix of agony, curiosity, and impatience to taste the limitless love he had the chance to taste for a second time.

Pam's look, her smile, and her fabulous body had affected his spirit and he was not able to think of the past and all those he had done to his partner. There was only one word that seemed to dominate in his mind. Sex, and she never said no, the only thing she needed was understanding and loyalty like everyone else in this world.

Pamela never lied to him, she was honest, and she didn't hide her feelings and enthusiasm when she first saw him. She was taken aback since he was different, but still, she liked him. She needed a partner, a good man, a loyal person who would never dump her. Additionally, she was eager to give him everything she had to make it work.

"Yes, baby, I am yours," Pamela said and she meant it.

They made love again and again, enjoying the summer solstice and they seemed relieved and happy they had gotten past their problems. They both liked watching the seagulls searching for the light during the magic sunset.

The weather was amazing; the puny air kept refreshing their exhausted bodies as the water carried on covering the thirst of living more intense erotic moments for the rest of their holidays.

It was the first time Michael was feeling so good; he didn't care for anything other than seeing Pamela happy and being naked all the time with her while having wild sex. He was indifferent to the other women, for Heidi and the rest of his ex-girlfriends because he had found the only one who would do anything for him. He had regretted and he would never betray her trust again. Serenity and tranquility had invaded his life and he was not naïve, he had found the treasure everyone was searching.

The moment she fixed her eyes on his, she realized she could do nothing to step back, she had fallen in love with Michael and she was happy about that, now she was sure no one could destroy their future, their relationship.

The Stranger

Chapter One

Do not lean against the door, it opens automatically.

After reading the sign, Elena loosened her shoulders and took a deep breath. She scratched her nose, trying to get used to the strange smell that was spreading in the railway carriage. A disturbing noise reached her ears as she gazed at an old woman eating chips in her seat, further back, in the railway carriage. She smiled at the woman and looked away.

Looking at her reflection, in the glass of the busy door, she pushed her red hair from her flawless face—she wore no makeup to hide her beauty. A couple of seconds later, she noticed a handsome man with beautiful blue eyes who fixed them on her. Elena, led by her curiosity, turned to look at the unknown man who, after that, started coming closer towards her. She tried to stay cool as the unknown, tall man with the well-shaped body and the nice haircut moved to the seat next to her. Without losing any time, she opened her bag and put on her sunglasses as her right hand was laid on her chest and her fingers started playing with the white buttons of her tiny, yellow shirt. She had no time to stay cool, she panicked.

Elena seemed annoyed but, on the other hand, she felt something burning in her body. He might be the pleasant surprise she was waiting for, since her breakdown, after her divorce from a man clueless of emotions, especially love and passion. Ten months had already passed since the tragic event and she sent those memories away from her mind. Miranda, her therapist, once told her, "Focus on you, satisfy your needs and leave all the nasty thoughts out of your life".

In the meantime, Elena was able to see another woman staring at the handsome man and she felt a bit weird. Emotions she had forgotten started rising again. *She is around twenty while I am forty. She has nice, blonde hair, nice lips while I have nothing. What am I thinking? I have no chance!* she thought and stopped wishing.

A middle-aged mother with her two kids stood up from their seats and moved towards the door. The children were holding tight onto their mother and she seemed so proud of them. Every time she smiled, they seemed so happy. Elena tried to release some space for the kids and their mother but after a bad trip she was found leaning towards the mysterious man.

"I am so sorry!"

The kind man smiled and nodded while he felt lucky since he could look at her face-to-face. However, Elena was shocked and moved away. She wasn't only shy, but she felt pretty surprised having such a man in front of her. He seemed like the dream guy from the Hollywood movies.

The unknown man didn't waste any time and, pretty soon, he was standing opposite her and staring at her dazzling beauty. He tried to be discrete since they had already attracted the passengers' interest. But he didn't miss the chance to turn his gaze to her at every turn.

Oh man, I need to talk to this woman... definitely. She is so beautiful, he thought a couple of minutes after his first estimation.

Elena was able to guess his thoughts, so she searched for the cell phone in her small, black bag—in a vain effort to seem indifferent—until a woman in black attire stood up from her seat to get off the train and Elena didn't waste any time. She went straight for the empty seat.

Lorene station was the place where most of the passengers disembarked and, in just a few minutes, the crowded train became an almost, empty vehicle for the rest.

Elena was now listening to music and staring at the empty seats wondering whether someone else would sit next to her.

Jeremy was supposed to get off the train since he had to go to work, but he decided to follow the 'femme fatale'. He trusted his instincts and he wouldn't give up. The confident man was decisive and nothing could stop him from getting what he wanted. Soon, he walked towards her while Elena followed every step he made. She could see his black shoes and his blue jeans but her glance didn't get any higher. She was looking at him as the strongest partner she could have ever had and, with no obvious explanation, she admired him. He had the absolute eroticism she was looking for and she realized that this was what she needed, a new love with a strong man who would satisfy all her needs. The way he decided to move made the anxious lady feel flattered but, also, scared since she'd been disappointed many times in the past and it would be devastating to face another failure. In less than a second, the handsome man sat down and gave it a shot.

"Hi! I'm Jeremy," he said, and sounded serious and determined to find out her name.

Elena accepted the surprise attack. Once again, she pulled away her long, red hair from her face and closed her phone. With a slight hesitation, and the aroma of his aftershave around her, she took off her sunglasses. Elena closed her eyes and thought of each and every moment of happiness she'd lost from her life. She'd forgotten the scent of a male close to her like that. Her brown eyes designated her bright face and were staring at his blue eyes without knowing how to react. Her eyebrows were quivering whereas two impatient, curious old ladies waited for her reaction while pretending to read their newspapers.

"I'm Elena," she said, and looked like a girl who had done something wrong.

Enthusiasm and impatience flooded the atmosphere but Jeremy had to do a lot more. He won her name but he had a lot of work to do as she could barely talk. Elena almost whispered her name and he was lucky enough to hear it. He stared at her sunglasses but his attention was caught by her silver nails. He had to say something to make her feel cool. The posters of the new campaign of Dior's sunglasses on the train doors gave him the chance to talk.

"I guess you like these sunglasses, too."

"Yes, I do!"

Elena sounded so sweet that they both smiled at the same time. As she saw his facial expression, she was sure she was wrong earlier. That man wasn't only handsome, he was just perfect and she would be crazy if she didn't allow herself the freedom to choose him. In no time, she put the sunglasses and phone back in her bag. Although, the noise of the railroad was loud, she wouldn't miss any of his words.

Her crossed legs mesmerized Jeremy who couldn't stop thinking the same thing again and again. Her heels awoke within him the fantasy he wanted to experience. *I want to be with her so much! I'm sure she feels the same.* Jeremy liked her hair and the way she said sorry when she fell on him. He loved her perfume scent.

The first thing Elena noticed, after his salutation, were the muscles in his arms and, beyond that, his deep voice which stirred up all her sensations. Meeting someone in his forties in great shape and handsome as well, doesn't happen every day, she thought.

"Nice to meet you, Elena..."

Jeremy couldn't take his eyes off her. The tiny, yellow shirt she wore left her belly uncovered while the silver chain which circled her waist stirred up his fantasy world. While he was looking at her dazzling body, his imagination ran through a path of satisfaction and passion for a single moment.

"Nice to meet you, too, Jeremy."

Elena knew exactly what it would follow. She had to make her decision. As a retired air hostess, she would keep annoying men at a distance, except for her ex, but this time it was different. She wasn't sure if she wanted to abstain from men anymore because, this time, she really liked him. He was handsome, very cool, and, according to her experiences, he was the hottest man she had ever seen. On the other hand, she couldn't ignore the fact that she was almost forty, and her abs were missing. Although she was a tall, vivacious woman capturing men's attention, Elena hated the moment he would see her naked. However, for her own good, and without any further thinking, she left behind her insecurities and joined the conversation.

"What's the time?"

"Who cares? I'm sure we have all the time we need to do everything."

Elena loved what she heard. Although, she had decided to deal with her apartment decorations, she postponed her plans. He was her interest now. Jeremy had style and she was impressed by the way he sounded. She had heard the same phrase again in the past, but no one had the energy and the confidence to support it like him. Elena smiled and seemed willing to follow Jeremy.

"I think the next station is for us."

He released his hands from his knees and moved towards the door. Elena looked at him and admired his well-shaped buttocks thinking how he would be without his jeans. She liked his white T-shirt and his aftershave scent. She liked him a lot.

In the meantime, Jeremy felt so self-confident. He stretched out his arm offering her his hand while Elena stood up and, with a huge surprise for all of them, including the two old women; she decided to take hold of his hand. The unpredictable woman smiled and whispered a word.

"Yes."

Chapter Two

In less than two minutes, Elena and Jeremy were standing on Marietta Street. It was Friday morning and everybody was out. The traffic was such a nightmare and the people on the streets were walking like maniacs. They were all in such a rush to arrive at work that no one talked and no one paid attention to what other people felt. The only description that fit the atmosphere was one of an unreasonable panic.

Jeremy looked at Elena and remained silent. He was trying to think of the best option they had to do something together but the sexy lady wasn't that patient.

"Now, what are we supposed to do?" she asked, and sounded hesitant to follow him.

Elena felt anxious and Jeremy had to do something immediately otherwise he would lose his chance. The mysterious woman started moving back and, soon, left Jeremy's hand. She felt shy and put her sunglasses on to hide her impulsiveness. She tied her jacket around her waist and, before saying a single word to back out of this situation, she heard him speak.

"Follow me."

His left hand slipped on her back leaving behind the anxiety and panic of the very first moments. Elena was still surprised but she did nothing to avoid him, she accepted his spontaneous move silently.

They came across an open market and its fussy atmosphere made them look at each other. Jeremy bought her a red rose and she felt like she was the luckiest woman in the world. He had just managed to help her get past her fears and insecurities.

After having fun with a group of tourists dressed in red, they found the way to reach a quiet path in which they could now see a huge, blue sign. It was the 'Blue Bird'.

Elena imagined exactly what this place was; feeling like it was nice and matched the scenery and their experience of the day. Blue Bird was a cheap hotel for those who needed a place to accommodate their passion for a while. The situation seemed totally dirty, and dangerously kinky, and that made her feel both enthusiasm and agony at the same time. The erotic thoughts and sexual tension she felt didn't let her realize that they were already standing outside of their dreamy room. She had never done something as wild and crazy as this before and she liked it.

"After you," he insisted, and she walked in silently.

Elena made the first step and he followed her inside the room. Jeremy closed the door and gave her a huge smile to make her feel comfortable. Elena seemed more content as she took off her sunglasses to see the white room. It had nothing more than a bed, a TV and a bath. The sheets were clean and the scent was nice. It was nothing special, but it was all they needed.

"You have no idea how much I want to make love to you," he said.

"What are you waiting for?" she asked.

Elena got the point as Jeremy tore off her shirt and started caressing her breasts while she was standing in front of the window. Her tiny piece of cloth landed on the floor and she grabbed his arms tightly feeling the passion he had for her. In no time, he tore her black bra off as well while at the same time she could do nothing but scream his name from her inflamed passions. The strong, decisive man kissed her lips with all his excitement and pressed his body on hers. Elena felt like a grenade which was ready to go off and only Jeremy was the one who could make her explode. She wanted to look at his eyes but he didn't give up his erotic game with her tits.

"This is the craziest thing I've ever done," she said, and seemed to enjoy every single moment.

Jeremy gave no answer and, instead of losing time with meaningless conversations, he began biting her nipples slightly. That was it! When he touched her with his fingers and started discovering her body, she froze forgetting emotions and just delivering her heart and her soul entirely to the unknown man. In a little while, Jeremy moved further down her body as he spread his kisses all over her skin. He could hear her breathing become more intense each time now that his lips were touching her body and that made him want to taste her beauty even more. He went further down and, in no time, he took off her blue jeans.

"Don't stop, Jeremy!" she almost begged him.

"I haven't started yet …."

Elena was speechless with delight. She was ready to faint from the exertion when he started pressing his body on hers and pushing himself against her until he was leading his partner to the wildest moments she'd never experienced.

The mysterious guy had found the way to treat women the way they wanted and Elena was absolutely sure that he must have seduced loads of women. It was the craziest experience she has ever lived and it was so hot that she wanted even more. When she saw the bed, she couldn't help but have him against her body. She liked the thought of having him on top of her body, lying on the bed instead of her toes. She wanted to please him as much as she could.

"Oh! Jeremy…."

The man stood up and took her in his arms. He put her on the bed and took off his white T-shirt. When Elena looked at his chest, she was almost ready to rush at him, but she didn't because Jeremy had already removed his pants and the surprised woman flirted with his desire. Admiration was the first impression he caught and that made him the happiest man in the world. He loved the way she was looking at him.

"You are amazing!" she said.

"You too, babe..."

Elena couldn't resist stealing his kisses. She felt there was no reason to resist. After all, she was an experienced woman who wanted to taste the pleasure of having the ideal male in her bed. Despite her salacious, always according to her belief, appearance she let herself be free and enjoyed every second. In a flash, she started licking his skin and her eyes were hooked on his desire. This made him even happier and more impatient. Surprisingly to him, Elena locked her lips on his and stared at him with burning passion. The following seconds she decided to act more seductively and started crawling up and down his body slowly. Her hands drove him crazy. She gave him the best erotic feeling he had ever experienced and, after her small gift, he realized that he wanted to have it all with this woman. Meanwhile, Elena was so obsessed with him that he had to pull her head away to release his mouth from her lips. The sexy lady felt so hot that she had no control of herself.

"Take it easy, babe, I'm here and I'm not going anywhere."

She couldn't speak, she just followed his moves and it was the first time, in her entire life, she accepted orders from a stranger. This guy managed to make her do everything he wanted with his kindness, strength, respect, and limitless confidence. He was what she had never met. Jeremy kissed her and lay on her. When Elena felt him on her flesh, she screamed with joy.

"I want you, I want you, babe." She had missed the feelings of the past when she cared about her physical needs and nothing more.

Jeremy smiled and started pressing his body on hers, driving her crazy. At the same time, he pulled the silver chain from her belly and, once again, she held tight to his chest.

"I want you now!"

"Yes!" he whispered and got in within a second. Elena liked what she heard and wanted to hear more.

"Oh! It's so good!"

Jeremy got off and Elena seemed surprised.

"What happened? Is everything okay?"

He gave no answer although her eyes were locked on him. The talented man got in and off again.

"You're killing me!"

He liked what he heard and she kept calling him with her eyes. The whole scene provoked her to stop thinking 'pink clouds forming big hearts'. She was ready to play his game. She had no intention to let him down since, sometimes, women want dirty games, too.

"You're amazing and I'll treat you the way you want."

"You are incredible!"

Elena couldn't do anything but scream. She didn't care for anyone but herself and the powerful moments she experienced. Once she pulled her hair back, she clawed at the sheets and held his back tight, having the need to feel his chest on her breasts.

"Do you like the way I love you?"

"I'm yours, babe, and I love your way!"

Jeremy kept seducing her body even harder while Elena threw the pillows off the bed and pulled at the sheets in order to keep her voice down since she was sure that the whole motel could hear her, but in vain.

"You are awesome, babe. Don't stop!" she exclaimed.

It was the best sex she had ever had and Jeremy's appearance made it obvious that he found her incredible. Elena flicked her hair on her back and then they rolled over with him now on his back in the bed. Now, it was his turn to scream.

***

"It was awesome!"

"Yeah, it was."

Elena couldn't take her eyes off him.

"You're amazing."

"And you're super talented."

Jeremy laughed while Elena squeezed his belly.

"I need a cigarette. Would you like one?"

"Yes."

She came back to the messy bed but she kept attracting glimpses of his admiration. He loved seeing her naked and she liked everything they did. They held each other as they quickly fell asleep.

***

The relieved man woke up as the evening passed into full night. The couple in the next room had a wild party and their noise made him laugh. Pretty soon, he realized where he was and what he had lived through a couple of hours earlier and, slowly, he began getting up from the bed. His body seemed so relaxed and his shoulders so loose that he felt amazing. He clasped his arms in front of his chest and walked towards the moonlight coming from the small window. As he stood there, he ran his hand through his black hair in an effort to fix the mess. Meanwhile, he tried to fix the curtains to let the moonlight come clearly in the room but the mechanism was broken. He left it like that and pulled the sheet away from his right foot to continue his stroll in the room. His nude body was trying to recover from the pleasant surprise.

Jeremy searched for the sexy lady. The bathroom door was closed but he got no answer when he called her name. In two seconds, he was able to see that her things, the small bag she had, her blue jacket, and her rest of her clothes were nowhere in the room. He knew she'd already left. A few steps further and he stood again in front of the window while he thought about what had happened. The moonlight rained down on his body and he was thinking of Elena. They had sex and nothing more. No future commitment, no future complaints, no future fights. For a moment, he liked that but, then again, she could have left behind her number or something to get in touch with her — if they both liked that idea—in the future. He searched for a letter, a card, or a piece of paper on which she might have written her phone number but nothing.

The first rain drops fell on the window and he realized that the moonlight was gone like the redhead woman. He understood he had to move on. Jeremy shook his head and fixed his hair with a smile of enthusiasm. He was lucky he had such an experience.

The bed sheets were still wet while the pillows were lying on the floor. He smelled his body and her perfume was still on him. He decided to stop thinking of her and tried to find his clothes while moving towards the bathroom. A shower would be perfect, he thought without losing any more time.

Fifteen minutes later, he was ready and left the room. The sounds and the screams he was listening to from the rooms down the pink hall, while walking towards the elevator, made him laugh and remembered their own screams and shouts.

The woman in the entrance of the Blue Bird looked at him leaving the motel and felt jealous of the woman with the red hair and the fancy sunglasses that left the building a couple of hours earlier. Further away, Elena couldn't believe what she had done. She felt so confused that the only thing she wanted to do was to run away from him. She hoped she would never see him again.

***

In the interval, Jeremy went to his restaurant in high spirits ready to do what he loved most. He wanted to cook for his customers and his good friends. As soon as he got in the small, crowded bistro he went straight ahead to the kitchen to see if everything was okay.

His place was decorated from his personal taste and reflected his personality. The bright colors of yellow and orange made it cozy while the red silks on the tables, and the colorful curtains on the large windows, turned the restaurant into a house meeting stop. At that moment, someone new came in and discovered the warm atmosphere and the delicious food.

The personnel had no problem in the kitchen and he went out to check on the rest of the stuff, dressed with his best, sincere smile and his pure, pleasant mood. The moment he was going to meet the new customer at the round table, in the yellow corner of his restaurant, he noticed the sunglasses he had seen earlier. He moved closer and managed to see Elena, lost in her thoughts and guiltiness, drinking a glass of red wine. She wore her jacket but she had caught her hair in a ponytail and sat staring at the crowd outside walking in the rain with their umbrellas. She admired the young couples running across the streets, neglecting all the noise and laughter from inside the restaurant.

"Would you like another glass of wine?" he said.

"No thank y...."

Elena seemed shocked. It was as if she came across a ghost. She started biting her lips while her fingers were completely lifeless resting against her glass on the wooden, round table. She had no idea how to react.

"You left without a note," he said.

"I...."

A young couple approached Jeremy. They both hugged him to thank him for the great dinner they had.

They both seemed nice and happy as well as willing to spread their love and kindness. In a little while, they left and Elena was ready to welcome his presence.

"Don't tell me that you work here," she said.

"Actually… this is my restaurant."

"That's great!" she was surprised.

"Yeah…."

They both felt like fish out of water and were catching the other customers' attention. Everybody knew Jeremy but no one knew the redhead.

"May I sit?" he asked.

"Yes, of course. Oh my God! I am so sorry."

"It's okay. By the way, I love your hair like that," he whispered.

"Thank you."

Elena couldn't take her eyes off him. She tried to act as if nothing had happened and decided to remain silent whereas Jeremy was holding his chin with his right hand, stealing glimpses of her. He couldn't explain the feelings he had for this woman. Body chemistry, he thought and Elena believed the same thing, too. They looked at each other, considering a new beginning, pretending nothing had happened between them.

"Would you like anything else?" he asked.

"No, thanks," she said.

"I could cook for you if you want." Elena smiled and, once again, she admired him for his behavior.

"You're very kind but I'm fine," she said.

"Okay."

The lady with the charming ponytail was in a lovely panic and couldn't stop thinking the same thing over and over again. *What does he want from me? I'm not a model. He could have any woman he would like.*

A decorative smile was always there not only on Elena but, also, on Jeremy's face. He was cool and nice but he, also, had his thoughts bothering his mind. *What's the problem with her? I must be doing something wrong. We had great sex and she seemed to enjoy everything!* He stopped his thoughts and returned back to reality.

"It was nice to see you again," she said.

"Let me take you home."

"I'll get a taxi.' Elena was nervous.

"Are you sure?"

"Yes" she said.

"Okay."

Jeremy stood up as Elena put her sunglasses inside her bag. She saw the disappointment in his eyes but she didn't know how to fix it. On the other hand, Jeremy couldn't do anything else since he acted as a gentleman. He had to respect her decision to leave by herself.

"Bye, Jeremy."

"Bye, Elena."

She went out of the restaurant, closing the door behind her, but she soon realized the biggest mistake she'd ever made in her life. He was the perfect match for her but her insecure ego destroyed everything. He couldn't be like her ex. Moreover, he was the one who gave her the best erotic moments of her life in less than an hour.

The rainy weather couldn't wake her up since she didn't have the strength to go back and apologize for her behavior. She was afraid to expose her feelings.

Behind the large, left window of the cozy restaurant, Jeremy kept looking at the sexy lady while all the customers were hooked on the scene. The patient man was there, acting nervously but ready to rush at her. He would do nothing without her consent although just a look would be fine for him to act on.

Elena was so curious about whether he was still there staring at her so she decided to have a glimpse for one last time. As soon as she did it, Jeremy made his move and, in less than a breath, he was there next to the sexy lady.

"You'll get wet," she said.

"So will you."

"I'm under the awnings of your restaurant. I feel safe for the time being," she said, and smiled.

His T-shirt got wet and his muscles made her remember the passion he spread on her body. She kept looking at him while Jeremy's view was captured by the silver chain hanging on her wet belly glowing like a treasure in the dark.

"Let's go."

"What...."

"Come with me...."

She found herself helpless to refuse and gave him her hand. It was so difficult to say no and she finally realized that it wasn't that easy for him to resist her presence.

They walked through the rain among the cars, which were stuck in a traffic jam, trying to avoid the anxious and in-a-hurry crowd with their umbrellas in hand. It was raining so much that Jeremy put his hands above her head to protect her. Spontaneously and, without hesitation, Elena hugged him as they both walked towards the subway.

Chapter Three

Green and gray were the colors of the crowded station, offering a depressive scene to the train passengers. A team of young women were laughing, taking off their jackets, whereas a small group of teenagers enjoyed the whole train experience.

Jeremy and Elena stood in front of the yellow line at the station sweeping the remaining raindrops from their hair and foreheads. The sexy lady held onto his chest with her right arm while the fingers of her left hand swept the water from his face. Her cuddling was so delicate and sensitive that it stole the crowd's attention immediately.

Jeremy kissed her hand as she looked him straight in his eyes. Although she was shy too, she let herself be free in front of the passengers, she came closer and closer as slowly as she could. The sound of her black heels provoked the glare of an old woman and she couldn't take her eyes off them. Elena hugged him and kissed the man deeply on his mouth. She had fallen for him the moment she had seen him.

"Don't you have somewhere else to go?" the old woman wondered.

"What was that whisper?" Elena asked.

"I've heard nothing," he said.

"Don't you have a home?" They heard again.

The old woman was ready to scold them for their behavior and Elena felt insulted. Jeremy was calm and, as a gentleman, he didn't cross the line of rudeness, even to indiscrete comments.

"You are right, miss. I promise we'll continue at home."

The old lady started staring at the teenagers while Elena looked proudly at her man, admiring his stance.

Jeremy felt her eyes penetrating his and considered himself lucky enough for his godsend. He fell for her too.

"Can you hear it?" He asked.

"What is it this time?"

"Listen…," he said.

The familiar sound on the railway became more intense.

"Our train….," Elena whispered.

"Exactly, miss beauty."

She fell for his body and he fell for hers. They got in the first gray passenger car without stopping their kissing. They acted so indifferent for the furious masses falling on them for an empty seat.

***

They felt so hot the moment they entered Jeremy's apartment, they closed the door and took their wet clothes off.

In no time, they were nearly naked and Elena was on top of him in his arms without bothering Jeremy as he walked towards the black, leather sofa placed in front of a large, white window. Her legs had circled his waist and she could feel him.

"What's that wonderful smell?" When they sat on the sofa, the white bottle on the small table didn't escape her sight.

"A drink I've made. Would you like some?" he asked.

"Of course, I'd love that!"

"Taste it," he said.

"Mmm… it's so sweet!"

Elena brought the bottle to her lips again and again expressing her enthusiasm. Jeremy was in heaven for his achievement.

"What is it? It's marvelous!" she said.

"It's a cream of chocolate and bourbon."

"It's fabulous," she said, and smiled.

"So are you."

Jeremy took the bottle and started raining her body with the tasteful cream. When Elena realized what he would do next she felt ready to scream. The dreamy man started licking her skin while the brown, sweet liquid flowed down....soon Elena felt his tension on her body and let his tongue taste the drink from her burning flesh. At some point, she couldn't deal with such a pressure and whispered as his helpless sexy victim.

"You'll drive me crazy with all these things you do to me.'

He smiled and continued. Jeremy was a genuine man and he knew how to make a woman happy with his own personality and his awesome sex abilities. Jeremy had his own way with women's satisfaction.

He licked her skin, then her breasts while moving downwards with his fingers on her nipples, ready to offer her an unforgettable night. This man had found the way to use his tongue and fingers appropriately. He knew exactly what to do. At the same time, Elena felt her skin chilling and begged him....

"I'm all yours. You can do whatever you want," she said.

"Patience, my love...."

When his face came near hers, she was ready to explode. The moment she felt his breath on her skin she was paralyzed, she felt amazing and she was sure she would never forget the time they first had sex, when she felt like a grenade.

"Oh! Please...."

Jeremy knelt on his knees and looked at her face. "Patience, my love...."

Soon, the sexy lady felt him inside her and released a breath of relief.

Jeremy left off kissing her for a while to enjoy himself and lay on her body. She grabbed and sucked on him offering a deep kiss to his lips. The confident man started dancing on her body and, in just a few seconds, she felt like never before.

"Honey, you're the sexiest thing I've ever met!"

Jeremy got off his knees and, moved to sit on the white, wooden table in the large living room.

"Sit on me, babe."

She loved the sound of their bodies slamming together and becoming one. Elena couldn't help but thank him for those ecstatic moments.

"Don't thank me, babe, it's my pleasure," he said.

"I'll thank you with my way".

Elena was so passionate to please him that she didn't even stop to take a breath. She loved caressing and scratching gently on his flesh while looking at his flushed face, now that they were about to come.

Jeremy enjoyed their meeting for the second time and rested his arms on the sofa. When she looked at him, they were both speechless. They seemed exhausted but they enjoyed every single moment.

Chapter Four

The exhausting night gave its place to the sunny day and Jeremy had already woken up. Elena was still sleeping on his bed and he kept gazing at her body. Her naked beauty was still attractive and the sunbeams on her back made it more seductive than ever. Elena wasn't a model but she was in good shape. Her curves were attractive and her figure was impressive.

The talented man let her sleep and walked towards the kitchen where he was about to make breakfast. By the time he'd finished, Elena came into the clean and tidy room. She liked the sight of a single man owning such a beautiful, clean, and organized house.

"Good morning!" she said.

"Hey… it's breakfast time."

Not only was he a great lover but, also, an independent man. The moment she saw him in the kitchen with the excellent smells, she was even more impressed. She adored him. He was the perfect match and she was thinking about that during the breakfast which was delicious.

"The breakfast is so tasty," Elena said.

"I'm glad you like it."

He looked at her as she avoided his look.

"Is there a problem?" he asked.

"Well… I just woke up. My face is without any makeup. Do you know that I'm forty?"

"So… I'm forty-three and I find you very attractive and beautiful," he said.

Jeremy disarmed her insecurities with his kindness. He smiled at her and Elena felt unique. She believed his words and she felt beautiful again after many months. With his last words, she stopped being hesitant and appreciated the gifts nature had offered to her so generously.

"Thanks for everything but now I have to go."

Elena stood up and, suddenly, felt his arm on her belly. She didn't want to push him; she didn't want to make him feel uncomfortable in his own house.

"Am I going to see you again?" he asked.

"That depends on you," she said.

"What do you mean?" Jeremy asked.

"I don't want to push you for anything. You'll decide if you want to see me again. As far as I'm concerned, I loved the moments we shared."

Jeremy felt good that he had followed his instinct. Elena wasn't just a sexy woman; she was a sexy lady who knew how to treat a man. She was honest with him and used no tricks to see him again.

"You know many things about me but I don't know anything about you." He said.

Elena grabbed the pen from the fridge and wrote her phone number and address on his memo.

"You can have my phone number."

She gave him a kiss and walked through the room to get ready. Jeremy followed her and got into the bedroom. He felt the need to get to know her better. He was so curious.

"Do you have any kids, Elena?" he asked.

"No, but I was about to make my own family with my ex."

"I'm divorced, too," he said.

"Do you have any children?" she asked.

"No."

Elena was fixing her hair when he came and cuddled her. She was wondering about his ex, but it wasn't the right moment to get deeper into his personal details. Besides that, all that mystery around him made him more interesting and, for the time being, that hot man was all she'd ever wanted.

"Why did you leave the motel without a note?" he asked.

"Cause I was afraid," she said.

"What do you mean?" Jeremy asked.

"I'd never done anything like that before and you seemed too good to be true." He kissed her and she fell into his hug.

"I have to go now," she said.

"I see." Jeremy sounded sad.

"Now, you know where to find me." Elena showed him her cell phone.

"Of course...."

Elena left his apartment capturing his figure inside her mind.

After her departure, Jeremy got in the shower and stayed under the hot water for several minutes thinking about his odd acquaintance. Two people, complete strangers a couple of days ago, became one sharing the same excitement.

***

As the hours passed by, morning became early afternoon. The sky was blue, there weren't any clouds and the temperature was high. The crowd in the streets had a pleasant mood and it was obvious it was going to be an interesting weekend for everyone.

There was eroticism all over the place. The women looked fabulous and well-dressed while the men didn't lose the chance to flirt in a nice and flattering way. A couple of girls had fun with three men joking around in the street corner. Another woman accepted a compliment for her short, red dress. Her smile was on her face during her walk to the club. When the door closed, it was lost and the lucky man rushed into the club.

In the meantime, Jeremy was in the kitchen of his restaurant preparing himself for the coming Saturday night. In a few hours, the entire place would host its loyal customers and everything should be perfect. The talented man had just finished the food garnish of the main menu when Janet came in the kitchen.

When should I call her? I don't want to scare her away. That was his main thought and his mind was already occupied by her figure.

"A customer wants to see the chef, boss," Janet said.

"Keep your voice down, Janet, we can hear you."

Michel came closer and realized that Jeremy hadn't heard a single word.

"What is it, Michel?" Jeremy asked.

"Janet called you, boss. A customer wants to see our chef."

"I heard nothing," Jeremy said.

"She almost screamed, boss," the young waitress said.

"Okay, thanks, Michel."

Michel went back to her work where she kept preparing the salads while Jeremy took his white hat and white plastic gloves off to meet the demanding customer. It was a due process for him. His customers would be served only the best. During his exit from the kitchen, he was still thinking of Elena and he decided to call her immediately after his conversation with the customer.

"Where is the customer, Janet?"

"It's the lady who's sitting in the yellow corner, boss."

Jeremy recognized the red ponytail and felt relieved. He went close to her and was surprised. Elena looked radiant with happiness.

"Good afternoon!"

"Good afternoon to you, too! How can I help you?" Elena smiled and so did Jeremy.

"You're so beautiful," he said.

"As you can see, makeup can do wonders!" Elena smiled.

"You don't need any makeup."

Elena shook her head and bit her lips while Jeremy was mesmerized by her eyes.

"What should I bring you?" he asked.

"There's a drink but I don't know its name."

Jeremy caught his chin pretending to be absolutely naïve.

"What kind of drink is that?" he asked.

"I think it's a cream of bourbon and chocolate," she said.

"I see. I'm afraid we have a problem."

"What do you mean?" Elena asked.

"That particular drink is only available at my place," he said.

"What are we waiting for?" she asked.

"Come and get it, then."

They kissed and left for his house. The erotic atmosphere surrounded the new couple.

"I hope you don't want me for my chocolate bourbon," he said.

"Oh, you caught me!"

They spent countless nights at his house enjoying endless moments of happiness and pleasure. That woman knew how to treat a man and her manners proved her admiration for him in every, possible way. On the other hand, Jeremy had found the appropriate way to make Elena feel safe and confident again while they both realized that being insecure, and uncertain of yourself, could lead to wrong paths of uncertain emotions and fake love.

They were made for loving one another and they did that for the rest of their lives.

Epilogue

Elena was lucky. She followed her heart and her instincts and managed to become the exception to the rule.

Rape is the most under-reported crime; 63% of sexual assaults are not reported to police.

Have fun but don't rush and always be careful, it makes the best combination both for men and women.

About A.A. Schenna

As a child, A.A dreamed of being a cardiac surgeon. Later, Schenna realized that this was not what he wanted.

Writing has always been his greatest pleasure. When he doesn't write action, adventure, romance stories or anything else, he reads everything.

Schenna admires all the writers he comes across and enjoys talking about books and magazines.

A.A loves meeting new people and discovering new places.

Trapped in Timelessness, Lake's Curse, The Alphas, Limitless Love Collection, On the Sixth Floor are available through the Solstice Publishing website.

Social Media Links:

Website: www.aaschenna.com

Facebook:
https://www.facebook.com/pages/AA-Schenna/701740166542505?ref=hl

Twitter: https://twitter.com/ASchenna

Acknowledgements:

To my dear editor-in-chief and good friend K.C Sprayberry, thank you for believing in me.

If you enjoyed this story, check out these other Solstice Publishing books by A.A. Schenna:

Can't Let Go

When Ralph met Sonya, he fell instantly in love. He did not know that she had a past, and that one day, that past would rise to haunt them both and try to tear their family apart forever.

http://bookgoodies.com/a/B0176WNIWG

Summer Thrills Summer Chills

The fear of being alone and lost. The nerves that come with starting over. Strange visitors. The sense that something, somehow, is off.

Plan to shiver. But not from the cold.

http://bookgoodies.com/a/B00YV0NZ84

Let's Have Fun Vol 3

A May/December romance, angels versus demons, and a plus sized woman who discovers love along with other great tales of the Summer Solstice.

Authors A.A. Schenna, Alex Pilalis, Jillian Chantal, J. Wayne Williams, Maighread MacKay, Margaret Egrot, Rachael Tamayo, Susan Lynn Solomon, Tevis Shkoda, and

Virginia Babcock delight you with stories from the longest day of the year.

http://bookgoodies.com/a/B01HBU1RQM

-

Adventures in Love

From a western gal in pursuit of the local sheriff to a single mom running a cooking show with her small children, romance blossoms in many situations. These wonderful stories prove that love is for all ages.

http://bookgoodies.com/a/B01BH2F7E8

A Winter Holiday Anthology

Enjoy these ten stories from a group of very talented authors. We celebrate the Winter Holidays around the world, brought to you by a multinational group of authors, with various traditions and one theme—joy and happiness.

http://bookgoodies.com/a/B017T6UJ8K

www.ingramcontent.com/pod-product-compliance
Lightning Source LLC
Chambersburg PA
CBHW070846030726
47504CB00005B/1236